"Christmas is 　　　　　　　　　　"

"Though I'm not big 　　　　　　　　　　
first one, let's do it 　　　　　　　　　　. While
we're in town, we'll grab lights—"

"Can we make all the ornaments?"

"Why not? Just add what supplies you need to our
list."

Jane laughed. "That list of yours is going to rival
Santa's."

"True." He reached for her, hovering his hands
midway between them.

Please touch me, hold me, her heart begged. More
than she needed any random item on his list, she
craved human contact—his contact. But was that
wrong?

For all she knew, she could be married.

Did that make her an awful person?

Dear Reader,

Most of my books tackle at least one heavy issue, but Jane and Gideon's story had so many that at times, while writing, I found my own pulse racing. Jane battles amnesia. One scene in particular tugged at my heartstrings—when she was in a department store, trying on clothes and didn't recognize the woman staring back at her in the mirror.

Enter Gideon. As a Navy SEAL, his entire life centers around helping others in need. But when he loses his leg in battle, he also faces an identity crisis—made all the worse when his wife leaves him because she doesn't want to be with a disabled man. Because of this, Gideon's emotionally scarred, believing no woman will ever again want him.

I fear many disabled veterans experience this same sense of loss. Gideon is one of the lucky ones who has forged a new life as a horse whisperer, fulfilling his need to help by nurturing emotionally scarred horses. But once Jane becomes a fixture in his home, he finds himself once again longing to help people—more specifically, her and her son.

I hope you enjoy this heartfelt read. More important, if you or anyone you know is a disabled vet, I pray for you to find your life's second chance.

Warmest wishes,

Laura Marie xoxo

THE COWBOY SEAL'S CHRISTMAS BABY

LAURA MARIE ALTOM

Recycling programs
for this product may
not exist in your area.

ISBN-13: 978-0-373-75782-4

The Cowboy SEAL's Christmas Baby

Printed in U.S.A.

Laura Marie Altom is a bestselling and award-winning author who has penned nearly fifty books. After college (go, Hogs!), Laura Marie did a brief stint as an interior designer before becoming a stay-at-home mom to boy-girl twins and a bonus son. Always an avid romance reader, she knew it was time to try her hand at writing when she found herself replotting the afternoon soaps.

When not immersed in her next story, Laura plays video games, tackles Mount Laundry and, of course, reads romance!

Laura loves hearing from readers at either PO Box 2074, Tulsa, OK 74101, or by email, balipalm@aol.com.

Love winning fun stuff? Check out lauramariealtom.com.

Books by Laura Marie Altom

Harlequin Western Romance

Cowboy SEALs

The SEAL's Miracle Baby
The Baby and the Cowboy SEAL
The SEAL's Second Chance Baby
The Cowboy SEAL's Jingle Bell Baby

Visit the Author Profile page
at Harlequin.com for more titles.

This story is dedicated to all disabled veterans
who have lost their way.
Please know you are loved
and appreciated by me.

Chapter One

Why was a baby crying?

Gaze narrowed, Gideon Snow hunched forward in his saddle. He tugged his cowboy hat's brim lower against the driving sleet's pinprick assault. At least twenty miles in on a sixty-mile trail through northern Arizona's Asuaguih mountain range, on an early December day fit for neither man nor beast, the last thing he should be hearing was an infant's wail. But there it was again.

Waaahuhah.

Had to be a fox.

No woman in her right mind would bring a baby out in this weather.

Jelly Bean, the pinto mare he'd been rehabilitating for a good twelve weeks, snorted. The cold had her exhalations wreathing her head in white.

"Good girl." Gideon leaned forward, smoothing his hand along her left cheek. She'd been through a lot—trapped in a burning barn during a Nevada sandstorm. Her fourteen-year-old owner died trying to save her. The girl's father had carried his lifeless daughter from the flames, then returned for the horse she loved. But the normally easygoing pinto charged into the heart of the storm. Three days after the girl's funeral, Jelly

Bean returned to what was left of the barn. It had taken six men to corral her into a trailer. Her coat had been ravaged by the storm. Her eyes filled with protective mucus.

It had taken Gideon a month of sweet talk to get near the poor creature, but once they'd turned the corner from strangers to friends, progress had been swift. Jelly Bean's owner prayed to keep the horse in the family as a living tribute to Angela.

This trail ride was Jelly Bean's final exam.

Gideon had waited for the ugliest conditions possible to push her to her limits. Tonight, he'd stop to make a campfire, and if she could once again handle being at a safe distance from flames, he'd know she was nearing the end of her stay with him.

Gideon would be sad to see her go.

Folks in this lonely corner of the world called him a horse whisperer, but at this point in his life, after all he'd been through, he figured it was the other way around. The horses helped him make sense of a life he no longer recognized as his own.

Was he angry? Hell, yes.

But that didn't change anything, and it sure as hell wouldn't bring back his wife or—

Waaaahhhuh!

Jelly Bean whinnied, turning her head toward the sound.

"What do you think, girl? Could there really be a baby out here, or is a crafty fox trying to get a piece of weekend action?"

Of course, the horse gave no answer.

The fact that Gideon had grown close enough to the mare that he'd halfway expected one told him it was high time he start talking to creatures other than horses.

But since he still couldn't stand being around people, maybe he should at least get a dog?

Another hundred yards down the steep, rocky trail, zigzagging around ponderosa pines and thick underbrush, landed Gideon in a clearing.

A blue dome-style tent flapped in the wind, and sure enough, from inside, there was no denying a baby's panicked wail.

Pumped with adrenaline, Gideon dismounted, loosely looped Jelly Bean's reins around the nearest pine trunk, then charged toward the infant. He ignored the mild discomfort in his left leg, but upon reaching the tent, he couldn't ignore the blood. The way it snapped him back to a time he'd fought hard to forget.

Blood pooled on the tent's floor.

It was everywhere.

And for a moment, red was all his eyes were capable of seeing. But then he forced his breathing to slow, shifting his gaze to the baby. The unconscious woman upon whose chest the infant shivered.

Holy shit...

Think, man...

For an instant, Gideon froze, taking it all in. The blood. The baby. The woman. The sleet's clatter on the nylon tent.

But then he sprang into action, ducking inside the shelter to check the woman's pulse. It was weak, but there.

Though getting a signal was a long shot, he unbuttoned his long duster coat and reached into his shirt pocket for his cell. As he'd assumed—zero bars.

He growled in frustration.

The contrast of the woman's long dark hair against her ghost-white complexion made her appear nearer death than life. A nasty bruise marred her otherwise flawless forehead. In Iraq, he'd grown too familiar with this sort of grisly scene. To find it again here, on this mountain he turned to for security and peace, was unacceptable.

He refused to succumb to the dark memories filling his dreams. Instead, for this woman and her baby—for himself—he had to fight.

First things first.

Triage. The baby's screams had grown frantic.

Gideon reached for the infant, who was half-covered by a sweatshirt. He lifted the newborn only to receive his next blow—the cord hadn't yet been cut.

Lord...

No need to panic. Women had been having babies for hundreds of years before fancy birthing suites ever existed. He'd make a fire to sterilize his knife, then do the deed.

He fully covered the infant, then exited the tent.

The red pool had darkened to rust, telling him the woman was at least somewhat stable since there was no additional fresh bleeding.

With the weather worsening, Gideon moved Jelly Bean beneath the shelter of a mammoth pine.

He unlatched his saddlebags, hanging them over his shoulder to carry back to the tent. Inside were dry clothes, a few first aid basics and fire-starting materials. There was also plenty of food and water, but no baby formula or bottles.

Back outside, he found another towering pine that was out of the horse's view, then assembled a small fire. His grandfather taught him the secret to making all-weather starting blocks that never failed to produce instant heat. Since the wood he'd dragged beneath the tree was wet, it took longer to catch, but soon enough crackling flames banished the cold.

For further insurance, he constructed a small lean-to made of sticks and pine boughs to put another layer of protection between his only heat source and the sleet.

The baby's wails drove him at a furious pace.

When they stopped, the silence, save for the sleet's clatter, came as a relief, but then terror struck. Had the infant died?

He charged into the tent, then froze.

The woman not only was awake, but held the infant to her breast.

SHE WAS BEYOND GROGGY.

Her eyes didn't want to open, but a primal instinct told her that if only for a short while, she had to tend to her son. After assuring herself of his safety, she could sleep, but he came first. Would always come first.

His cries ripped at her heart.

Though she barely had strength to draw her next breath, she somehow knew he was hungry. She fumbled with her jogging suit's zipper, and then raised the hems of her T-shirt and sports bra. Breast bared, she guided her baby to his first meal. Luck was with her when he greedily latched on.

Relief brought tears.

Eyes closed, she finally found the energy to wonder where she was. And why. How come she couldn't remember anything other than the most basic of all urges to stay alive?

She licked her lips, desperate for water, when the tent flap that had been fluttering in the storm's wind opened farther.

A giant of a man stepped in.

She screamed.

He kept coming.

He wore a black cowboy hat and boots and a long duster-style coat of the sort she'd only seen in old Westerns. Could he be a hallucination?

He held up his hands. "I'm here to help."

Could she believe him? She didn't know, and clutched her newborn closer. What was wrong with her? Why was her mind blank?

"Woman, you gave me a helluva scare. What landed you all the way out here? How'd you get that nasty bump to your head?"

So many questions. She had answers for none. "I—I don't know."

Brow furrowed, he knelt alongside her. "What do you mean you don't know? What's your name? Where's your baby's father? What kind of man lets the mother of his child go camping in this weather?"

"I don't know. *I don't know.*" Fighting back tears, she shook her head. "D-do you have water?"

"Of course. Be right back."

Sleet fell so hard on the flimsy tent that it was collecting on the sides, causing the nylon to bow. Moments later, when the cowboy stooped to enter, he punched at both sagging sides before unscrewing the lid on a gallon jug of water. He handed it to her, but then understanding dawned on his whisker-stubbled face when her arms proved too weak to leave her baby.

He got down next to her, holding the jug to her lips. In the process, the backs of his fingers touched her chin. For an instant, they warmed her cold skin. The sudden heat made her shiver.

She then grew hyperaware of the man's size.

And the vulnerable position she and her newborn son were in.

How had she landed herself in this predicament? Nothing made sense. The man raised valid questions. Where was her baby's father? Why did her mind feel numb?

She drank deeply of the cowboy's gift.

The water might as well have been liquid ambrosia sliding down her throat. Never had anything tasted so good.

Eyes closed, she drank until feeling as if she couldn't hold any more. The whole while, the man patiently knelt beside her, holding the heavy jug.

"Can't recall ever seeing a woman drink that much," he said. "Guessing you were dehydrated?"

"I'm sure." She shivered.

Her baby unlatched and cried, kneading tiny fists against her right breast. Maternal instinct had her shifting him to her other side. When he drew milk, a hormonal flood raised a knot in her throat and had her eyes tearing.

What could have landed her in this situation? Why did her head feel like a blank sheet of paper?

"Since it's not getting any warmer," he said, "once you finish with—" the man gestured to her nursing baby "—you know, give me a holler and I'll bring you a rag and pot of hot water. We need to get you both cleaned up, then cut the baby's cord."

"You know how?"

"Had some EMT training. Not much, but you've already tackled the worst. As soon as this weather clears and you feel able, we'll get you to a hospital."

She nodded. Something about his take-charge demeanor, the gentle yet confident note in his voice, eased her worry. She wasn't sure what she'd done to deserve it, but by what could only be the grace of God, she and her baby were in capable hands.

"How are you doing?" Gideon stroked Jelly Bean's cheek.

For the past hour, he'd prepared pot after pot of melted sleet that he'd then delivered to the mystery woman—along with a T-shirt for her to use as a rag. While waiting for the latest batch to boil, Gideon tended to the horse.

"Bet you never thought we'd encounter a newborn and her momma, huh?"

The horse snorted, then stilled, closing her eyes while appreciating his affection.

"Damned if this doesn't beat anything I've ever seen." Gideon kept his voice a low murmur for only the horse to hear. Over the past months, he'd learned Jelly Bean calmed whenever he was speaking. Maybe her former young owner had been a chatterbox? Regardless, since he rarely had anyone around his place besides his nearest neighbor, Mrs. Gentry, it was good to have someone to talk to—even if that *someone* was a horse.

He continued stroking, combing her mane.

Did the mystery woman need help with her long hair?

The crown of her head was matted. Leaves and small twigs had caught in the longer sections.

"I'd have offered to brush it for her," he said to the horse, "but that might be overstepping, you know? Although I'd be at a loss to come up with a more bizarre situation. Hope you're up for a long, slow ride back to the cabin."

Gideon figured once the weather improved, he'd get

the woman and her baby settled on Jelly Bean. He had misgivings about entrusting the skittish mare with such precious cargo, but there was no other choice. Upon reaching his place—or, if he got a signal in the high mountain meadow—he'd call for help. "Until then," he said to the horse, "we're on our own."

He removed Jelly Bean's saddle and blanket, then brushed her down. Fed her a few handfuls of feed, then picked his way over the treacherous ground back to the fire.

Now that the woman and baby were as clean as could be expected, he could no longer put off cutting the infant's cord.

After slicing three inches of nylon from each of his bootlaces, he chucked both pieces into the pot, along with his best bowie knife. This was hardly a sterile environment, but he'd do his best to ward off infection.

Smoke from the fire rolled out from under its shelter, filling the temporary camp with a sweet-smelling normalcy that couldn't be further from the truth.

In all his time with the Navy SEALs, he'd never encountered anyone with amnesia. It was unsettling.

While the water came to a rolling boil, minutes ticked by.

He pretended to know what he was doing, but now that he'd tossed cordage and his knife into the pot, how did he get it all out while maintaining sterility?

The only logical conclusion was to let the water somewhat cool, pour some out to wash his hands, then pluck out the cord and knife. If he didn't touch the blade, the procedure should be no big deal.

He put the heavy cast-iron lid on the pot to keep sleet from getting in, then used his coat sleeve for a hot mitt to heft the pot from the fire.

Gideon trudged back to the tent, and since he couldn't exactly knock on a tent wall, he stood outside, clearing his throat. "You decent?"

"Almost."

He glanced beyond the tent's flap and caught flashes. Her creamy-skinned collarbone. Long dark hair swinging like a curtain over her cheeks before she swept it behind her ears. Her breasts' pale underbellies.

She glanced up.

For a heartbeat, her piercing clover-green stare locked with his. Feeling part rescuer, part voyeur, he lowered his own gaze.

Sleet fell harder. Thunder rolled.

"You okay for me to cut the cord?" Gideon tugged his hat brim lower against the sleet's assault.

"Please. Come in." Her voice barely rose above nature's racket. She'd cleaned herself and her baby, but the tent floor was still a mess. "I guess now's as good a time as any since my son is sleepy from his meal."

"Yeah." *My son.* Gideon hadn't even thought to ask. In another world, he'd longed for a son. Now he knew better. His time in the Navy had left him reactionary. Trapped in a crisis loop. He fixed impossible situations. A long time ago, broken people. Now, horses. Still a good thing, right? But according to his ex, his capacity to genuinely care? To give a shit? He'd left that ability in Iraq along with his— No.

Not going there today.

He stepped into the tent, then poured hot water over one hand, then the other, letting the runoff flow onto the already-wet floor.

"This should only take a sec." He tried conveying a sense of calm that was a bald-faced lie considering the pounding of his heart.

Lightning cracked. Thunder boomed.

Sleet fell hard enough to make the tent's ceiling appear as if it were writhing.

"This can't be good," the woman mumbled.

"Nope." Gideon set down the pot to check on their sole means of transportation. Careful not to touch his freshly rinsed hands, he used his elbow to nudge the tent flap back to check on Jelly Bean.

"What are you looking for?" the woman asked.

"A horse. Or, in other words, our ride out of here."

"Is he okay?" She gingerly sat up.

"Kind of hard to tell."

"Why?"

"*She's* gone…"

Chapter Two

"Sorry." The man set the cast-iron pot alongside her, then headed back into the storm. "But I've got to find the horse. You're too weak to walk out of here, and—"

"Go. I'm fine. No need to explain." And there wasn't. She might not be able to remember her name, but she knew enough to realize Mother Nature wasn't doing them any favors. The faster the man found their ride, the better.

Once he'd gone, leaving her alone again with her panic, minutes seemed stretched into hours.

What if he was hurt, and she was on her own again? Instinct told her she was a strong woman. If she'd survived giving birth in a tent, she'd somehow make her way back to civilization. But it would sure be a whole lot easier with a friend—not that she and the cowboy could be called friends.

She didn't even know his name.

But she wanted to.

She eyed the pot he'd set beside her and lifted the lid. Beneath a thin layer of water were two nylon strings and a mean-looking knife. Everything needed for her to cut her son's cord herself. Once they were separated, she could bundle him, then help her new friend find his horse.

Her backpack was within reach, so she tugged it closer, taking a travel-size bottle of hand sanitizer from the front pocket. How could she have known it was there, yet not know her name or who'd fathered her child?

None of this made sense.

Her runaway pulse made her breaths choppy.

Lightning stabbed the earth with enough force to make her jump. Where was the cowboy? He shouldn't be out in this weather.

Operating with newfound urgency, she exposed her son's tummy, then enough of her own abdomen as low as she could comfortably reach. She squirted hand sanitizer into her palms, rubbed them together, then tied one nylon string roughly two inches from her baby's navel. She recalled reading about this procedure and knew there were no nerves in the cord, which is why cutting it didn't hurt. Doctors clamped it to prevent bleeding. The string would serve essentially the same purpose. She made quick work of tying the second string as low as physically possible, then took the knife from the pot, careful to touch only the bone handle.

Drawing her lower lip into her mouth, she clamped down with her teeth, then made the first cut. The knife was sharp, easily cutting the cord. The second cut was completed as smoothly and while she might have expected to feel a certain melancholy, her current drive to save the stranger who had saved her overrode sentimentality.

Before her son's delivery, she'd had the forethought to make a pallet of clothes. Those were blood-soaked and ruined. She'd covered herself and the baby with more clothes.

Now she rose, eyeing the stranger's saddlebags that he'd left inside the tent.

Darkness was falling too fast, making the lightning flashes all the more disturbing.

She swaddled the thankfully still-sleeping baby in a dry sweatshirt, then used the pot's remaining warm water to wash herself. There were clean undergarments and a jogging suit in her backpack, so after bathing, she hurried to dress before her teeth chattered out of her head. Her long hair was a nuisance. Hands trembling from the cold, she finger-combed the tangles and leaves, then braided it, fastening it with a ponytail holder she'd instinctively known was in her backpack.

The tent floor resembled a crime scene.

After drinking more water and eating a protein bar, she rolled the entire mess into the floor tarp she'd spread, wadded it into a ball, then flung it outside.

She next unrolled her down sleeping bag and tucked the baby inside.

From the stranger's saddlebags, she borrowed a red long-sleeved flannel shirt. Teeth still chattering, she lost no time in pulling it on.

She found a ball cap in her pack, as well as a plastic pouch containing a foul-weather poncho. Dizzy from the energy she'd expended, she ate a second protein bar, drank a bottled sports drink, then forced a deep breath before ducking out into the storm.

"JELLY BEAN!" GIDEON CLIMBED ONTO a boulder, only to slide back down. "I swear to God once I find you, you're headed straight for the glue factory." Of course, that would never happen, but in the heat of the moment, the notion deserved consideration.

Thankfully, the sleet had eased up.

The thunder and lightning moved on.

In this part of the country if you didn't like the weather, all you had to do was stick around ten minutes and it would most likely change. In the higher elevations, snow had already set in, closing the trails and passes.

He spent another thirty minutes circling the camp's perimeter, but felt obligated not to venture too much farther. With luck, Jelly Bean would return on her own. Without luck? She'd either show up back at the barn or become bear or mountain lion bait. The grim fact forced him to increase his pace.

"*Jelly!* Where the hell are you, girl?"

He rubbed his left thigh. For the most part, he was one of the lucky ones. His old war wound only reared its ugly head when he overexerted himself or when fronts rolled through. He had friends who'd been to hell and back fighting two wars. One in the Middle East, and another once they got home, battling pills and depression.

A lot of times, Gideon found himself missing the camaraderie of being around his SEAL brothers, but as for the work itself? Never.

"Hello? *Sir!*"

Gideon frowned.

What was the woman doing out of her tent? He had enough to deal with in rescuing the damned horse. If she went and did something even more stupid than traipsing out into the woods to deliver her baby? Say, like falling and breaking her leg or neck? Then what? He'd be stuck carrying her and the baby home. He rescued. That's what he did. But that didn't mean he had to like it.

Framing his mouth with his hands, he shouted, "Over here!"

In the Navy, his call sign had been Angel. He'd hated

it—especially after his injury. Because most days, he felt chased by demons that left him feeling anything but angelic. He was angry. Depressed. Pissed at his ex. None of which he could do anything about, which was why his new life of solitude suited him just fine.

He resented this woman for intruding on his privacy. If it weren't for her, Jelly Bean might have had a successful test run. On the flip side, better to have found out she still wasn't at 100 percent now, rather than when she carried an inexperienced rider.

"There you are."

"Here I am." He rounded a corner of the trail to find her looking like one of those yellow toy bathtub ducks in her foul-weather gear. "Why aren't you with your baby?"

"I'm rescuing you."

He snorted. She'd barely made it fifteen yards from the tent, well within easy earshot to hear if her son made so much as a whimper.

"Any luck finding your horse?"

"Does it look like it?"

"What's got you so salty?"

"I'm not," he lied. "I'm just worried about how we're going to get you out of here."

"Give me a day to rest up, and we'll hike." Her hopeful half smile blinded like staring too long into the sun. He blinked. "I'm not sure how, but I remember feeling most at home outdoors. That must be why I came all the way out here even though I was pregnant. Maybe the fall that conked my head brought on my labor?"

His gaze narrowed. "Wait a minute… If you're out here without your baby, does that mean you cut his cord?"

She nodded.

"I'm impressed." He really was. She might be loony, but she had spunk. He admired that in a woman.

She waved off his compliment. "I cleaned that mess in the tent, too, but I'm feeling woozy. Now that I know you're all right, would you mind if I joined my son in taking a nap?"

"Not at all. Hell, I might grab some shut-eye, too. In my own sleeping bag, of course."

"Of course." Her cheeks reddened to an adorable degree. *Adorable* wasn't the sort of term he typically bandied about, but for her, it fit.

He held her arm while traversing the last bit of steep trail. He told himself he would have done the same for anyone, but would he? Something about her both annoyed and fascinated him.

"Mind if I ask you something?" she said.

"Depends." Touchy-feely wasn't his thing.

"Relax, cowboy." She covered her mouth while yawning. "I was only going to ask your name."

He couldn't help but chuckle, then paused to extend his hand. "Gideon Snow."

"Nice to meet you." When she pressed her small, cold hand against his, if he hadn't known better, he could have sworn his heart skipped a beat. Stupid. Corny. Inappropriate. "Wish I had a name to call you. For now," he said, "let's call you Jane. You know? Like Jane Doe."

She winced. "That's not very original."

"True. But I'm guessing you've got family out there missing you. Probably even a husband."

She'd withdrawn her hand, and now inspected her empty left-hand ring finger. "I don't feel married."

Good. Because for some inane, selfish, inexplicable reason, he didn't want her tied to another man. But then considering what a mess she'd made of Gideon's day that made no sense. Logically, he should have been thrilled to have her and her baby be someone else's problem.

The trail widened, and they finished the short walk side by side. The sleet had stopped, but the whole forest sounded as if it were dripping.

A crow's sharp call rose above the melting sleet's patter.

"Is it just me," Jane asked with a shiver, "or is it getting colder?"

"It is," he said, glad for the distraction from wondering how such a pint-sized woman had found the wherewithal to not only give birth in the forest, but then cut her baby's umbilical cord before chasing out into the storm.

She was really something.

Not that it mattered.

Gideon wasn't in the market for female company. That ship had sailed long ago. His contentious divorce guaranteed he'd never again climb aboard the *Love Boat*.

Chapter Three

"That was delicious. Thank you." Jane couldn't recall the last time she'd enjoyed a meal more. But then considering the fact that she didn't know her own name, was that a surprise? The act of eating proved especially enjoyable, because of the normalcy of sharing a meal. If only for a moment, it distracted her from her frightening reality—of literally having zero reality.

"It was no biggie." Her cowboy had added water to a packet of dehydrated sweet-and-sour pork. He was right; the shared feast hadn't required an inordinate amount of culinary skill, but it was hot and filling and for now, that was good enough.

Before sundown, he'd built up the fire, then moved the tent closer to take advantage of the radiant heat.

Jane cradled her son, rubbing the underside of her chin along his downy hair. Part of her couldn't wait to get him back to civilization. Another part was terrified of what that return might find. There had to have been a reason for her to have endangered herself by traipsing off into the woods this late in her pregnancy. It had been not only irresponsible, but just plain dumb. She was lucky they were still alive.

So why had she done it? A nagging voice told her she didn't want to know.

"Do you have kids?" she asked Gideon, eager to change the subject—if only in her own mind.

"Nope."

"I'm assuming you're not married?"

"Nope."

"Would you ever want to be?"

"Nope."

"Why so fast to respond?" She kissed the crown of her baby's head. "I've only been a mother for a few hours, but this guy's already got me wrapped around both of his tiny pinkie fingers."

"Let's just say I've been there, done that, and learned the hard way that marriage isn't for me. The only logical conclusion is that parenthood would end with the same dismal results." He set the foil food packet on the ground beside his log seat, then warmed his hands in front of the fire. He was tall and ruggedly appealing, but not traditionally handsome. His nose was crooked as if it may have been broken. His jaw was too wide and his cheekbones too high. That said, something about the way firelight danced in his brown eyes called to mind s'mores and made her wonder what kind of ugly breakup had resulted in such a bad attitude toward any sort of new relationship.

Skirting the direct issue, but still curious, she said, "Tell me about your parents."

"Not much to tell." He added a log to the fire. "They've passed."

"Sorry."

He shrugged, staring into the dancing flames. "They were hardly the sort who inspired procreation or family unity. I'd never even celebrated Thanksgiving until joining the Navy. Before Mom split, we did usually have Christmas."

"That's sad. But back to your grim outlook on marriage, what happened?"

"Aren't you tired?"

"Yes, but I won't get a wink of sleep until you answer my question."

He sighed. "If you must know, I'm divorced. My marriage ended so badly that my ex wanted her freedom even more than my assets. We had to have set a record for the world's fastest split."

Jane whistled. "Did you cheat on her?"

"Why would you assume that?"

"You said you were in the Navy. I thought you might have had a girl in every port."

"I didn't." He pitched a log into the fire hard enough to send sparks flying.

"I believe you. Sorry."

"Apology accepted. How about you turn in. I'll keep watch."

"For what? Mountain lions? Bigfoot?"

"Look…" He clasped his hands. "Don't take this personally, but I'd rather sleep outside."

"Oh." Why did his rejection hit her as if he'd turned down her invite to a Sadie Hawkins dance? "Sure. I understand."

But she didn't.

Worse yet, it wasn't so much his rejection that had her super confused, but her silly reaction. For a woman who literally knew only two people in the world, to have one dismiss her stung.

GIDEON WOULD HAVE enjoyed nothing more than stretching out in his sleeping bag in Jane's toasty tent. The night had turned breezy, and his fingers and nose felt cold enough to snap off. Just what he needed: to also be missing his nose. That'd be a big hit with the ladies.

Suddenly mad at the world, his ex, Missy, and most of all himself, Gideon kicked dirt into the fire.

Nights were always tough.

Jane's incessant babbling and questions weren't making this particular night any easier.

How long had it been since he'd shared a meal?

The part of their time when they'd exchanged small talk about favorite old movies had actually been pleasant. He would have never pegged her for an old-school sci-fi fan. Maybe once they got back to his cabin, he'd make popcorn. The two of them—make that three—could settle in for a movie marathon.

Stop.

He pressed the heels of his hands over his stinging eyes.

For the sake of argument, even if he was interested in hooking up, perky Jane was hardly his type. He was willing to bet that somewhere out there she had a husband desperately searching for her and their son.

Gideon would be wise to adopt his usual protector role, get her and her son safely delivered back to her family, then wash his hands of the whole situation.

In fact, as well as Jane had already recovered from giving birth, he figured Jelly Bean needed him more than she did.

"Gideon?" she called from the tent.

"Yeah?"

"What was that noise?"

"I didn't hear anything."

"Listen! It's like a snort, then I heard a twig snapping. Maybe even a growl."

Gideon heard nothing but the occasional owl and wind high in the pines.

"Could you please stay in here with us? Otherwise, I don't think I'll get a wink of sleep."

It was her second time using the phrase. Had it occurred to her that if she stopped winking long enough to close her mouth and eyes that sleep might come? Shaking his head, Gideon banked the fire, then snatched up his sleeping bag. If Jane wanted him to stretch out alongside her, rather than spending his night upright on a log, who was he to argue?

Hours later, Gideon woke to golden sun warming his face.

Even better? The mesmerizing sight of Jane breast-feeding her son. Witnessing the nurturing act warmed a long-frozen place in his heart. But then he grew fully awake. Fully grounded in the knowledge that if his heart ever did thaw, it would be as gray and ruined as freezer-burned meat.

The woman was pretty, but the expression on her face when she held her baby transformed her into what he could only describe as ethereal. Then she turned to look at him.

Her faint smile faded to fear.

As if she'd forgotten he was even there, she looked up with a startled jolt. "G-good morning."

"Hey."

The few minutes it took for him rummage around in his bag, straightening his prosthetic without her seeing, took a lifetime. He couldn't get away from her fast enough.

She apparently wished the same.

"Um…" Because he'd been on more pleasant bombing raids, he cleared his throat. "Give me a sec to get coffee in my system and I'll launch a fresh search for the horse."

She nodded. "I've got freeze-dried scrambled eggs if you'd like me to make breakfast?"

"Thanks. But you've got your hands full. I'll tackle chow. You handle baby maintenance—speaking of which, he probably needs a fresh diaper." Lord help him, now that he was on a roll, he couldn't shut up. "I've got biodegradable paper towels that should work."

"Thanks."

"No problem." He unzipped his sleeping bag, then rolled onto his knees, maneuvering himself into a standing crouch that his height forced him to use all the way to the tent's zippered door.

"You slept in your boots?"

Gideon froze. "Is that a problem?"

"No. I mean, I guess not. It's just a little odd."

"I don't recall asking your opinion." The blunt-edged statement had been intended to shut her up. It did. But instead of feeling satisfied, he felt ashamed.

Of course, she had no way of knowing he'd slept with his boots on for the purely prideful reason of keeping his most carefully guarded secret.

"Sorry." Her ghost of a smile as she rubbed her son's back should have warmed him, but it only served as a further reminder of his condition. Of the reason his entire life had fallen apart. "I was teasing. It's touching—the fact that you care so much about protecting us that you fell asleep fully dressed. Thank you."

Gideon grunted before tugging hard enough on the tent's zipper to make the whole structure lean.

He had to get out of here.

Being around Jane and her baby only served as a reminder of the life he might have had.

He was one of the lucky ones. No pain. Full functionality. But somehow in the grand scheme of things, none of that mattered.

Some days he felt as if that grenade hadn't just taken his leg, but his man card.

What he needed to feel better was to get Jane and her baby off his mountain. He'd help find her family, and that would be that. Like his ex, she'd be a memory best forgotten.

Outside, gulping fresh air, he made quick work of tossing her the paper towels, then starting a fire.

When the camp soon smelled of sweet woodsmoke, brewing coffee and dehydrated eggs mixed with onions and peppers, his stomach growled.

But then Jane emerged from the tent, carrying her son, spoiling not only his privacy, but his peace.

Gideon consoled himself by reasoning that within a few hours, Jane would no doubt have the cavalry out searching for her and her baby boy. When they found them, Gideon would once again be blessedly alone.

He was great with that.

Had to be.

Before his mind took any further control over his day, he cleared his throat, then gestured to her half of breakfast. "Eat up. Coffee's almost done."

"Thank you." She ate from a neon-green plastic bowl she'd unearthed the previous night from her pack. It was the type of pricey camping frill that weekend trail rats would find necessary when the only purpose it served was adding extra supply weight. Gideon ate his freeze-dried meals straight out of the package. If he hadn't had a horse, his cast iron pot weighed too much for hiking. But it was a luxury for cooking over a decent-sized campfire.

"Sadly, I'm off caffeine until I'm no longer eating and drinking for two." She kissed her tiny son's cheek—practically the only part of him visible past his thick sweatshirt swaddling. "But this sure is good. Thank you."

"You're welcome."

"You're spoiling me." She nodded toward the bowl she'd rested on her knee. "But I'm not complaining. I get the feeling I've always enjoyed camping. Fresh air, wide-open spaces. The sharp scent of pines contrasting with sweet woodsmoke…" She punctuated her words with yet another faint smile. For someone who literally could have died not twenty-four hours earlier, she was awfully chatty. "Listen to me yammering on. Maybe I was a poet?"

"Doubt it. Not with all your fancy gear." Finished with his meal, he chucked the waste in a plastic trash bag.

"Was that sarcasm, cowboy?"

"Not at all. But think about it. From your tent to your backpack to your bowl and fork—all REI or some other big-name sporting goods chain. Camping gear like that doesn't come cheap. At the very least, we know you had a comfortable amount of disposable income."

Her smile faded. "But what does that mean?"

He shrugged before using his shirtsleeve as a hot pad to take an old-fashioned percolator from the fire. Morning coffee usually smelled and tasted better on the trail, but today, Gideon feared no amount of caffeine or ambience would help his suddenly sour mood.

"You were the one who said it."

"It was an observation. Nothing more." After setting the coffee atop a stump remaining from turn-of-the-century timber cuts, he ducked into the tent, rummaging through his saddlebags for sugar. Some guys liked their beer. Others enjoyed smoking or myriad other vices. Gideon didn't just like sugar, he needed it. And since he had plenty of friends with worse habits, he didn't even try abstaining.

"Guessing you've got a sweet tooth?" Jane said after he'd removed the grounds from the percolator, flinging them into the weeds, then dumped a good portion of his sugar into the remaining black liquid.

Ignoring her, he found a stick to use for a stirring spoon.

"I'm just messing with you. No need to turn grumpy."

"You sure are perky for a woman who's lost."

"But see? Since you found me, I'm not really lost at all." Her words proved braver than the unshed tears shimmering in her gaze.

"Never mind. Sorry I brought it up."

"It is a valid observation." Her tone turned low and introspective. "Maybe we can use it to find a clue about who I am?"

"I'll play along." Gideon sipped more coffee.

"Hmm…" Her smile returned. "What kinds of jobs require a perky demeanor?"

"Kindergarten teacher?"

"Yes—but if I were a teacher, how would I have had time for a leisurely hike in the middle of a school day? Today is Thursday, right?"

"Wait—how can you know the day of the week, but not your own name?"

"Great question. I suppose I could have been on maternity leave?"

"True. But even if that were the case, I still don't get why any pregnant woman would have been out for a strenuous hike in less than ideal conditions. It doesn't make sense."

"I know, right?" Her shoulders slumped, as if too many of her own questions left her deflated.

If he'd had a heart, he would have felt sorry for her. But honestly? Most days he had no emotions at all. He finished the coffee, then wiped the pot and its workings dry with a shop rag he kept stashed in his bags.

Once he'd finished, and she hadn't budged from her spot on a log, Gideon cleared his throat. "You mentioned yesterday that you'd need a day of rest before we head back to civilization. But earlier, you looked like you're getting around okay to me. How about we pack up and at least try going a few miles?" When she didn't answer, he found himself blabbering on. "If you do—get tired—we can always stop and make camp. I just figure it would probably be best if…" *If I were no longer around you and your baby.*

The two reminded him too much of all he'd lost—correction, all his ex had thrown away.

"Sure. I'll help pack."

"Thanks, but I'd feel better if you and the baby stay by the fire."

"I don't mind."

I do. After five minutes of bickering, Gideon finally convinced Jane that her energy would be best utilized on the hike out. He spent the better part of the next hour packing. In a perfect world, he'd have let the collapsed tent air-dry before folding and then rolling it, but there was no time.

As soon as they reached his cabin, he'd drive her and her son into town, drop them at the hospital, then he'd never see either again. Maybe he'd get lucky and catch a cell signal in that high mountain meadow where he'd once picked up an Arizona Cardinals game. Then he could call for help and let authorities sort out Jane's mess.

Yes—that was by far the better option.

As his ex had so thoughtfully reminded him, he wasn't fit to be around women or children.

Chapter Four

Jane.

She somehow knew she'd never been a fan of the name.

She had almost as hard a time thinking of herself by that moniker as she was traversing the steep trail while keeping a safe hold on her son. Her cowboy companion had offered to hold her baby, but she'd politely declined. In a brain and heart filled with fog, the one thing she did know was that she fiercely loved her newborn and wasn't letting him go.

Gideon had called the baby John—as in John Doe, but that was no good, either. She held him snug against her chest and while pausing to catch her breath, Jane sneaked a peek beneath the sweatshirt she'd wrapped him in. *Chip.* Because he looked sweet enough to be a chocolate chip. The name as well as the reasoning would probably be silly to anyone else. But to her? It worked.

She paused, dragging in gallons of sweet-smelling mountain air. As nasty as the previous day had been, this day was sunny and while not exactly warm, at least above freezing. Birdsong came as a welcome change from the sound of clattering sleet.

"You okay?" the cowboy called from a good thirty feet up the trail. He not only carried her large-framed hiking pack, but his saddle bags. The exertion didn't seem to affect him.

"Sort of?" She managed a faint, breathless smile.

"Do we need to rest?"

"Would you mind?"

"Not at all." He glanced forward on the trail, then back to her. They'd only been hiking a couple hours, yet her body felt as if she'd run a marathon.

You did give birth twenty-four hours ago.

The same voice justifying her exhaustion left an underlying wave of not really fear, but a vague sense of unease. As if laziness wasn't approved—regardless of the excuse.

Excuses are for wimps.

This new voice served as an intimidating reminder that she hailed from hearty stock. She was no quitter and had apparently been taught from a young age that nothing good came without plenty of hard work.

"Hey..."

Jane glanced up to find Gideon now in front of her.

"You don't look so hot." He reached out, almost as if he'd intended to touch her arm, but then changed his mind. "Are you tired? Or did you remember something?"

"I'm not sure. Maybe both." She trudged a few feet farther to a flat boulder, backing onto it.

"Tell me what's going on." He removed both of his loads, then sat beside her. After digging through the nearest pack for a canteen, he unscrewed the lid, offering it to her.

"Thanks." She drank deeply, resisting the urge to lean against him for physical and emotional support. He was a stranger, yet at this moment, she knew him better than she knew herself. "I just had the strangest sensation—not really a memory, but a gut-deep feeling that someone in my life wouldn't approve of me taking a break."

"Your husband?"

She glanced at her ring-free left hand. "I-I don't think so. Maybe my father?" She passed Gideon the canteen.

"If you feel I'm pushing you too hard, we can stop here for the night. I was hoping to make it farther—to a creek where we can replenish our water supplies. But if—"

"I'm okay," she promised. "Just needed to catch my breath."

"How's the little guy?" He nodded toward the baby. He'd again started to reach out, but as earlier, she got the impression that Gideon didn't want to touch. Why? Was he afraid of overstepping personal boundaries? Or getting too close? Given the fact that in a day or two they'd never see each other again, it was unlikely they'd ever be more than casual acquaintances. A good thing, considering her tenuous grasp on reality.

"He's great. Sleeps a lot. But I guess that's to be expected?"

"No clue." Gideon toyed with the canteen lid. "Babies aren't my thing."

"What do you do? I've been so caught up in my own mystery that I hardly know anything about you."

"Not much to know." He took another swig of water, then offered it to her.

"Tell me about the horse that ran off. Do you think he's all warm and cozy back in your barn?" She drank deeply. It felt odd—the intimacy of their lips touching the same vessel.

"Hard to say. And *he* is a *she*." Gideon shared the horse's heartbreaking story.

After hearing about what the poor creature had been through, Jane said, "We have to find her."

"Let's get you and the baby to a hospital first. Odds are, she is back at my place. If not, I'll come back out as soon as you two are safe."

"But—"

"Not up for debate." When Jane again tried speaking, he held out his hand to stop her. The gesture royally ticked her off. As if another man in her life had a nasty habit of shushing her.

"Don't do that again."

"Do what?" He was rummaging through his pack.

"Shut me up. I'll say my mind whenever I see fit." Her raised voice woke the baby.

Her son showed his displeasure with a series of fitful cries.

"Don't blame me for that." Eyeing the infant, Gideon raised his hands in the universal sign of not guilty. "All I was trying to do was impress upon you the urgency of getting you and your son back to civilization. This time of year, snowfalls are epic, and we're way past due for a big one. Hopefully, the horse can fend for herself."

Jane jiggled her son, but that only made him cry louder. "Do you think he's hungry?"

"How would I know?"

"You seem to know everything else," she snapped.

He sighed. "I'll give you privacy. Why don't you…" He gestured toward her chest.

"Feed my son? With my *breasts*? Are you twelve?"

"What happened to perky Jane? I liked her way better than snarky Jane."

Jane rolled her gaze skyward. "I liked you better before you were so bossy."

The baby wailed.

"I'm out of here to look for signs of the horse, but I'll stay within earshot. Holler when you're done and we'll go together to the stream, then set up camp for the night."

"Aye-aye, Captain Bossy."

When he turned his back, Jane stuck out her tongue.

While she was by no means an expert on infant care, thankfully, breastfeeding was coming naturally to her and her sweet little Chip.

With him feeding, Jane arched her neck back, drinking in warm sun. All of this was so strange. Part of her felt wholly at ease in the forest. Another part warred with the notion that beyond a few hunches about who she was, and what sort of lifestyle she preferred, the truth was that where her memories should be now yawned a frightening black hole.

She knew she preferred Gideon's sweeter side as opposed to this new grouch. And she also knew that given her aversion to his demanding tone, she was now apprehensive about what secrets her former life may hold. Could she have been on the run from someone abusive? Or just a bad breakup from her baby's father?

She may not know much, but she somehow knew she didn't love Chip's dad.

But what if I'm still married to him?

As much as she wanted to fill in the missing pieces of her life, another part of her was afraid. What if she didn't like the woman she turned out to be?

The question made her pulse race uncomfortably fast.

So much so that the logical choice for her immediate future seemed to be remaining with a grumpy cowboy. What was that old saying about it being better to be with the devil you knew? Not that Gideon was in any way mean or cruel, but given his current frame of mind he could hardly be considered warm and fuzzy.

Tears stung her eyes, but she swiped them away.

She needed to be strong.

Not just for the baby, but herself. This was no time for a breakdown. Whatever had led her to run into this forest, she feared she'd need all her strength to face it.

A twig snapped.

She darted her gaze in that general direction. "What was that?" she asked her son. "Probably a squirrel, right?"

He stared up at her with enormous baby blues.

"But it sounded bigger. What do you think?"

There was another twig snap. A low huff.

Jane froze. "Maybe it's Gideon's missing horse?" Standing, holding her son close while he finished brunch, she called, "Jelly Bean, sweetie? Is that you?"

A low growl came from the camp's edge.

Not thinking, just doing, Jane screamed, *"Gideon!"*

GIDEON HEARD JANE'S cry and abandoned the track he'd been following to run toward her and the baby.

"Jane?" he called. "Hang tight! I'm coming!"

After damn near breaking his neck while charging through thick underbrush, Gideon finally reached the trail, then poured on extra speed to reach the boulder where he'd left her.

Pebbles skittered after him on a steep downhill section.

He rounded a corner to find her standing with her zippered jacket hanging open and full breasts exposed save for the parts covered by her still-nursing son.

As fast as he'd been running, Gideon now screeched to a full stop, politely averting his gaze.

"Thank goodness you're back," she said as if she wasn't standing there half-naked. "There's a monster growling—just over there." She pointed to the dense woods behind them. "I thought it was Jelly Bean, but then whatever it was turned bloodthirsty."

"Bloodthirsty?" He nodded. "Guess it could have been a mountain lion, but they're usually fairly skittish, and aren't known for making warning noises before they eat you." He winked, then realized her condition. "Would you, ah, mind fastening that up?"

A glance down left her cheeks reddening while she fumbled to hold her now-sleeping son and fasten her front-latching sports bra. Turns out it couldn't be done, so she returned to her rock seat, setting her son alongside her. Once she'd closed the "mess hall," she looked Gideon's way.

He'd meant to turn his back to her, but hadn't quite managed. He'd intended to offer to hold her son for her, too, but the words refused to leave his mouth. So there he stood. Frozen. Like a big, dumb rock.

Above her, a squirrel chattered.

"Apparently," she said, "he's bothered by the sight of a little skin, too?"

"I'm not bothered," Gideon said, "just figured you might be cold." He averted his gaze. "Are you decent?"

"I was *decent* before, but if you mean fully clothed—yes."

"Sorry." He sighed, then found the wherewithal to once again meet her gaze. "Your scream got me spooked. Then I showed up and you were—well, barely dressed."

"Because I was feeding my baby."

"Yeah, I know that now. Give me a minute, okay?

It's not an everyday thing around here for me to find pregnant ladies on my trail."

"I'm not pregnant anymore," she sassed.

"By God, you are a handful." He raked his fingers through his shaggy hair.

"Sorry, I'm not sorry?" Now she winked.

Gideon busted out laughing.

And then she was laughing.

The racket startled her baby awake, but then she was smiling down at him, and rocking him, and crooning soft words to coax him back to sleep.

Something inside Gideon shifted.

Instead of viewing the two of them as enemies hellbent on destroying his carefully structured life, he recognized them as something far more menacing—*enjoyable*. They represented a welcome change. A bright spot of hope in the dark fog that had become his world.

But there was danger in that hope, because just as soon as he returned Jane to the real world, her family would claim her. Her *husband* would claim her. And just like that, Gideon would be in the dark again.

The funny thing was, he'd been there so long, he'd almost convinced himself he liked it. But then this spitfire had come along, changing everything.

"What's got you so deep in thought?" she asked.

"You." He hadn't meant to tell the truth, but it had slipped out.

"Is that good or bad?"

In keeping with his truthful scheme, he said, "A little of both. I'm sorry."

"For what?" She hugged her baby close, kissing the crown of his head. He'd seen her perform the maternal move at least a dozen times, yet it never failed to stir him. He could deny it all he wanted, but he realized he wasn't mad at his wife for stealing the joy of becoming a father from him. He was mad at himself.

He waved off her question. "It's way too deep to go into now. We're strangers. I'll try being nicer and leave it at that."

Eyes narrowed, she cocked her head. "Sometimes strangers are best for making confessions. The beauty of them is that you get to unload, and then never see the person again."

"True. But then your juicy secret is out there, just waiting to hit tabloids and TMZ."

"Interesting…" Gaze narrowed, she said, "I wouldn't have taken you for the TMZ type."

"I'm not." He sat beside her to dig into his saddle bag. "But a few of the younger guys I served with never stopped yapping about Hollywood crap."

"You're a veteran?"

"Yeah." He pulled out two protein bars and handed her one.

"Which branch?"

"Navy. Has anyone in your family serv—"

Her complexion paled.

"Sorry." Gideon gave himself a mental kick. Dumbass. If she couldn't remember her own name, how was she supposed to remember a family member's service records?

"No worries." She ran her thumb over the protein bar's label. "Chocolate chip. Did I mention that while we were hiking, that's what I decided to name my son?"

"Chocolate Chip? Cute." Gideon bit into his bar and chewed. "Don't think I've ever met one."

"You have now. Chip for everyday. Chocolate for holidays and special occasions." She smiled.

He smiled.

It was all very civilized, but underneath these new-found manners ran a tension Gideon couldn't quite get a read on.

They sat in silence long enough for the songs of nature to feel noisy in Gideon's head. Wind in the pines. A cawing crow. He wanted to say so much to Jane, but wasn't sure how—or even why. The sensation was as unnerving as it was unwelcome.

"Ready to get going?" he asked. "I'd like to make the stream in a few hours, then set up camp well before nightfall."

"Sure." She wadded up her bar's wrapper, tucking it into a pocket of her pack.

He liked that she hadn't littered. He liked her green eyes that reminded him of new grass in the spring. He liked her laugh and the way she doted on her son.

He did not like the way she'd unwittingly taken over his life.

Which was why, once they'd gotten back under way, he set the pace faster than he probably should, because he had to escape not only Jane, but the biting pain of what it felt like to be connected to another person. And to know with absolute certainty that he'd never see her again.

IT TOOK HOURS to reach the gurgling stream beside which Gideon was now assembling Jane's tent.

She sat on a fallen log, nursing her son, appreciating the unseasonably warm late-afternoon sun. It was almost as hard to predict Arizona weather as it was Gideon's moods.

At one point during their death march out of these woods, he'd seemed downright chivalrous, waiting for her to catch up. He'd almost held her hand over an especially rocky part of the trail. But at the last moment— as if remembering girls have cooties—he'd changed his mind.

Her stomach growled.

"Gideon!"

"Yeah?"

"Mind if I have another one of your protein bars?"

"Go for it."

"Thanks." Midway through the day, he'd removed his coat. She had spent hours staring at the back of his green T-shirt. How had it escaped her that his shoulders were broad, his hips narrow, and his derriere... *Oh my.*

Might her former self have giggled at such an observation? The fact that she didn't know soured her stomach.

He cursed at her tent. "This thing was clearly designed for yuppies."

"I'm not a yuppie." She bristled more at his tone than the label. She honestly wasn't even sure what being a yuppie entailed.

"But that's the thing." He straightened. "You don't know. Your gear shows that you have a more than average knowledge of backpacking. Almost as if you were in training for, I don't know? Something big—like the Pacific Crest Trail."

Free hand on her hip, she cocked her head. "Me? Hiking from Mexico to Canada? Yeah. I suppose that's possible. But if that was the case, what am I doing in Arizona?"

"I just said you could be in training. The trail we're on is a notorious killer."

"Good to know."

"Have you been all through your backpack? Are you

sure there's nothing we could use for a clue? How could you not have at least had a credit card or ID?"

"No clue. Maybe it fell? Or I was in such a hurry to get started I left it in the car? When we stopped by that mushroom patch, I had to dig deep for the paper towels. I didn't see a single useful item in regard to discovering my identity."

"No worries. We'll figure it out. In fact, once we get you to a hospital to get checked, I'm sure the place will be crawling with your family."

"Hope so..." Tears stung her eyes, but she swiped them away. This was no time for a breakdown. Whatever issue had led her to run into this forest, she feared she'd need all her strength to face.

With Chip fed, she got herself zipped up, settled him on a soft grassy patch, then dived into Gideon's saddlebags for the protein bar.

She easily found it, but she'd also stumbled across a laminated photo she had a feeling Gideon would never want her to see. It had to have been taken at his wedding. He wore Navy dress whites, and the woman's fullskirted gown seemed too fancy for the casual beach setting. His look of adoration for his bride made Jane's stomach tighten.

Was this the woman who had broken him?

Of course, there were always two sides to every story, but what part had he played in their marriage's collapse?

"Mind helping me out with the center pole? I don't know how the hell you got this assembled while in labor. It's like freakin' origami."

She tucked the photo back in the saddlebag, then went to help. "You have to work it through. You can't just shove it. The whole process needs finesse."

"Words to live by."

It took her a minute, but then she caught his grin and blushed. "You know what I mean. Here, let me show you."

"Do I need to cover Chip's tender eyes?"

"Stop." She brushed past him to grab hold of the channel the tent pole needed to be worked through. Now that she had an audience, the motion did feel less than wholesome in a comical way.

When Gideon stepped in to help, Jane fought to ignore the tingly awareness stemming from his faintest contact. He reached over her, raising the nylon channel for her to feed the pole through. The action was simple, so why did her every move strike her as beyond complicated? The heat of his chest radiated against her backside, and when his forearms accidentally grazed the sides of her overly sensitive breasts, she bit her lip to keep from begging for more.

Insanity! That's what this was.

Her brain got the message, but her body refused to listen.

Ten minutes later, she stood side by side with Gideon while surveying their work.

"We have a home," he said of their blue abode.

Home. An interesting choice of wording given their situation. She felt the same vibe—at least in the moment. The setting with its gurgling stream and sunny glade surrounded by towering ponderosa pines was idyllic. The stuff of fairy tales. Only by all logical standards, her current situation more closely resembled a nightmare.

Only…it didn't.

Now that Gideon had mellowed, and her son seemed healthy and content, and she was immersed in a postcard-worthy setting, her current lot in life no longer seemed all bad.

"What's causing that smile?" Gideon asked.

"Oddly enough, the fact that this trek has suddenly turned kinda fun." She smiled.

"You won't be thinking that when this clear sky causes nighttime temps to dip into the twenties."

"That's why Chip and I have you—to build us a nice, toasty fire."

"True..." He returned her smile, warming her from the inside out. "But please remember that my whole rescuer gig is only temporary. As soon as we hit civilization, you and your little chipmunk will be history."

His comment should have brought her comfort, but all it really did was make her feel like crying.

Chapter Five

"Aw, why are you crying?" Gideon supposed the decent thing to do would be to draw Jane into a nice big hug. But while they'd had fun joking around while assembling the tent, that didn't mean they were best buddies or that he'd ever again be decent. What went down in Iraq had fundamentally changed him to the point that he was no longer a nice man. Missy, his wife, had told him every chance she'd gotten before she'd left him.

Then she'd died.

Her words had stuck to his skin like a shirt with static cling.

Jane said, "Y-you have this way of making me feel like I'm on an emotional roller coaster. One minute, we're laughing and everything's chill. The next, you look at me and Chip as if we're your mortal enemies. My gut tells me you're a great guy, but your mean mouth is telling a different story."

"Damn, woman…" Summoning a half smile, he pressed his hand over his heart. "I've had gunshot wounds hurt less."

"Don't act like you don't know what I'm talking about—and why are you carrying around a wedding photo? Sorry—I saw it by accident, but it doesn't fit with the man I've come to know."

"Look…" Needing a barrier between them, he crossed his arms and took a defensive step back. "I keep that pic to remind me I'm never again taking that route. As for what's going down between us? I'm trying to be a stand-up guy. I promised to get you and your son safely to a hospital and I will, but beyond that?" He shrugged.

"I stupidly thought we were friends."

"We're acquaintances. Nothing more. Psychologically, I'm guessing you're placing importance on our relationship, because at the moment, aside from your infant son, I'm literally all you have." He softened his voice. "That won't last forever. In fact, there are probably search parties out looking for you right now."

"Think so?"

He nodded.

She looked so utterly lost, so confused and alone and beaten, that he broke his every rule to extend his arms to her for a quick hug. When she stepped into his embrace, crying so hard that tears wet through his T-shirt, there was nothing he could do but hold her. Which hurt him. Every second she sobbed against his chest equated to weeks—hell, maybe months—it would take him to rebuild his carefully constructed walls.

How long had it been since he'd felt needed? He used to thrive on problem-solving. A part of him craved charging in to Jane's rescue, but to fully embrace her needs, he'd have to abandon his own.

Or maybe not? Maybe all this situation required was basic human compassion. What could it hurt to at least offer her that?

She sniffed, finally backing away. "Sorry. I-I guess you're right. I've been putting on this brave front, trying to act upbeat and like my loss of memory doesn't really matter, but it does. I'm terrified. I have dozens more questions than answers. Biggest of all? What if I ran into the woods to escape danger?"

"Not gonna lie—" with her no longer in his arms, he missed their physical connection "—it's a possibility. How about if we make a deal—once we get to the hospital, and your husband or parents step forward, if you feel at all threatened, give me a sign. Tug your ear or scratch your nose."

"Then what?"

"No clue. We'll figure it out when the time comes."

"Promise?" She'd lowered her gaze, and when she glanced up at him with late-afternoon sun making her still-teary eyes glisten, Gideon was lost.

"Sure." By this time tomorrow, Jane and her son would be back with her family, and he would be reunited with Jelly Bean, who was no doubt miffed to find he hadn't yet made it home. His life would have officially reverted to normal.

His neighbor and occasional caretaker, Mrs. Gentry, would barge in right when he sat down to dinner, yammering on about what naughty boys and girls his rag-tag crew of livestock had been. After helping herself to a good portion of his meal, she'd then devour most of his dessert, leaving him even more grouchy than when she'd arrived.

"You're scowling again." Jane had left him to retrieve Chip from his grassy patch in the sun.

"It's not about you. I have a busybody neighbor who makes me all kinds of crazy. I was just thinking about how infuriating it is when she eats my baked goods."

"I'll have you know I'm the best baker in—" She covered her mouth when a gleeful laugh bubbled free. "Did you hear that? I'm not sure how I know, or even where I stash my prized pink KitchenAid mixer, but I know I'm a baker—and I like pink."

"This is good," he said, collecting wood for a fire. "Is anything else coming to mind? Do you specialize in pies or cake or cookies? Please, God, let it be cookies." His laugh felt shockingly good—and real. As real as his love for oatmeal scotchies and snickerdoodles.

"I'm not sure. Maybe? That might make sense since the first name that popped into my head for this little guy was Chip."

"That's a logical assumption. And shoot, I never met a cookie I didn't like. I'll bet you make them for gifts—you know, for your family and neighbors." He dumped his latest load of wood next to the stone ring he'd previously made.

"That sounds nice."

"Yes, it does."

Call him crazy, but relief shimmered through him over the fact that her mood had returned to her formerly perky self. He liked her better smiley than moping. A double standard considering his own mood swings over the course of their journey. But now that they'd cleared the air between them, and he'd had his say about the fact that they were destined to be acquaintances—nothing more—his spirit felt lighter. With her not expecting anything from him, he felt more at ease.

Groundwork had been laid.

Rules of engagement firmly established.

"Thank you." On her tiptoes, she pressed a sweet kiss to his cheek. It was no big deal. So why did his skin feel as hot as if he'd been branded?

"You're welcome," he said, "although I'm not sure what for. Regardless, no more of that, okay?"

"Of what?"

"You're going to make me spell it out? That kiss, Jane. No more of that."

"Don't be silly." She waved off his concern. "That wasn't a real kiss. *If* I ever decided to really, truly lay one on you? I would hope you'd recognize the difference."

JANE HADN'T MEANT to kiss Gideon. Just like she didn't mean to flirt. But somehow their conversations naturally took that turn. Unlike him, she decided not to stress over it. Since she didn't have a whole lot else going for her, what could a smidge of harmless flirtation hurt?

Plenty!

Her conscience was all too quick to remind her of the very real possibility that she could be married. But if that was the case, why didn't she feel as if she'd made a lifelong commitment to the love of her life? Wouldn't she at least have a vague recollection of such a momentous event?

Chip grew fitful, so while Gideon was off gathering more firewood, Jane ducked into the tent to feed her son.

The smell inside made her happy.

It was a comforting, somehow familiar scent—sunbaked nylon and the sweet smoky remains of countless campfires. The tent was large enough for three or four people. Why would she have packed such a large tent for only herself? Could she have had a friend, and they'd been injured?

Outside, the tumbling crash of firewood being dropped onto the growing woodpile made her call, "Gideon!"

"What's wrong? Is the baby—oh." He ducked into

the tent. Upon catching a flash of her bare breasts, he blanched, then backed out. "Jane, we talked about that, too."

"Sorry." She drew a sweatshirt over herself and the baby for modesty. "I was so excited to run something past you that I forgot Chip was still nursing. Isn't it wild? How a couple of days ago, I knew nothing about being a mom, yet now, I feel as if this precious guy has always been in my life."

"That's great," he said with a hint of annoyance, voice muffled from having turned his back on her. "But what did you call me over for? You sounded as if it were urgent."

"It is." She explained her theory about the oversize tent.

"What do you think? Could I have been with someone else when I set off for my hike?"

"I guess it's possible." He scratched his head. "That theory's just as plausible as anything else."

"I thought so, too. But then that would mean someone else is out here—lost and hurt. Should we hike back to where you found me to check for any additional clues?"

"No. We stick to the plan. Get you and the baby to a hospital, then let professionals handle it from there."

"O-okay."

"What?" He looked back. "I'm growing way too familiar with that look of yours."

"I'm tired of dead ends. When will one of our theories pan out?"

"In due time. Relax."

"How?"

"I don't often share this—hell, I haven't even thought

of it in years. But back in my swinging single days, I was known for giving magic massages."

"Yeah?" She couldn't help but laugh.

"Yuk it up. After cooking dinner, I was going to offer you one of my top-secret, patented shoulder rubs, but if you don't want one, I—"

"Oh—I never said that. In fact, just as soon as Chip's finished his meal, let's go ahead and have ours. I'm excited to gain firsthand knowledge of your supposed skills."

"That's what all the ladies used to say." Through the open tent flap, she watched him walk toward his impressive fire pit. The way he filled out his Wranglers was mighty impressive, too.

This more playful side of him was a charmer.

Jane closed her eyes, imagining a young Gideon, fresh out of basic training, out for a good time on a Friday night. Was he like this all the time back then? Unfettered by the emotional baggage that now seemed to have him on constant guard? What happened to him? Would she ever know?

Chip had finished, so Jane began the now-familiar task of closing her bra and other garments. She set the baby on top of her sleeping bag that she'd already rolled out, then dug into her pack for freeze-dried dinner packets to prepare.

She called to Gideon, "Craving beef stroganoff or chicken and rice?"

"Neither!" he said above the noise of his hatchet biting into a small downed pine. She glanced over her shoulder to find he'd removed his shirt and slung it over his shoulder. He'd worked up a sweat. His chest and washboard abs glistened in the sun.

Oh my. Her mouth went dry.

If she was a married woman, she shouldn't be this attracted to a stranger. Yet there it was—an undeniable visceral pull toward this cowboy who'd saved her and her baby's lives.

Determined to turn her focus to anything more productive, she worked on changing Chip's makeshift diaper. What she wouldn't give for a box of premoistened wipes…

She made do with the remains of her water bottle and a wad of paper towels, then swaddled him in preparation for cooler temperatures once the sun dipped below the neighboring mountain range.

Outside the tent, she found that Gideon thankfully was clothed, only his black leather cowboy hat didn't exactly detract from his looks while he started the fire. Soon, woodsmoke flavored the air, and he'd rigged a tri-pole wooden support frame for his cast-iron pot.

"You're really good at all of this." She perched on one of the logs he'd dragged next to the fire.

"Given the right tools, anyone could do it."

"Not according to some of the reality-style survival shows I've seen."

"Oh, yeah?" Still working, he rounded in front of her, giving her an up-front view of his powerful thighs and that Wrangler-clad behind. Cue her wild pulse. She licked her lips. This wasn't good. "Do you remember being an armchair fan of that sort of thing?"

"No clue. But I guess I'd have to be if it's coming to mind. It just seems like making a fire doesn't come as easy to most people as it does to you."

He shrugged.

"You never told me what you did in the Navy."

"This and that." He added a log to the fire.

"Did you do 'this and that' on a sub? An aircraft carrier?"

"I was a SEAL. My team and I pretty much did whatever needed doing. End of story."

"Wait—aren't SEALs the crazy ones you see all the time on the news? Like you're the guys who presidents go to when they want bad guys captured but for no one to know about it, right?"

He winced. "Something like that."

"So you're basically the premium-deluxe model soldier?"

"Give it a rest. What were my meal choices again?"

"Why are you out here when you could be doing your military thing? You had to have trained forever to land that kind of gig. Why quit now? You're so young."

A muscle tightened in his jaw. "I'm going to get more wood."

"We have lots."

"Don't you get it? I need to get away from you and your damn questions."

His harsh tone pushed the air from her lungs, but that didn't hurt as much as the sight of him walking away. Throat aching with tears, she refused to cry over the jerk.

If shadows weren't growing longer by the minute, she'd have taken off herself. But she didn't have just her own safety to consider. With darkness transforming deep greens to ominous gray, Jane had no choice but to remain by the fire.

He was an ass.

He should never have gotten all bent out of shape over Jane's questions. They'd been harmless conversation starters. So why had he acted as if she'd asked him to spill state secrets?

Given the physical toll the day had already taken, Gideon pushed himself harder than he should have to reach the rock outcropping that was at least a thousand feet above their camp. It would be hell getting down in the dark, but he didn't care.

All that mattered was escaping the forest's gloom.

He needed wide-open sky to breathe.

He marched up, up, up until breaking past the tree line, rocks clattering in resistance to the nearly vertical grade. But then he arrived, stepping out onto a jutting ledge that afforded a view of mountains and trees and enough orange-and-lavender-streaked sky to almost make him believe himself back at sea. Or in some god-forsaken desert where his life had at least had purpose.

Now he saved horses, and that was a good thing. But it wasn't the same. He used to be an integral part of a kick-ass team that literally saved the world.

He'd prevented rogue nukes from entering the US. He'd stopped terrorists from using chemical weapons on entire cities. He'd rescued ambassadors and ordinary US citizens from situations labeled impossible. He and his team had done it all under a cloak of anonymity, and he'd loved every second of his service.

When he hadn't been on a mission, he'd been training on base in San Diego, or loving his wife, Missy. They'd talked incessantly about having kids, but they'd put off starting their family because the timing hadn't been right or they hadn't had enough money saved or Missy was afraid of going into labor with him away on a mission. With the benefit of hindsight, all of that was BS.

They should have had babies—lots. Boys and girls and dogs and cats and hamsters. His world could have been an embarrassing bounty of emotional riches—even after losing his leg. But his pride had killed all of that—both figuratively and literally. That said, he wouldn't shoulder all the blame. They'd both played roles in their marriage's end.

He knew in his mind that Missy's death had been an accident. When she'd passed, he hadn't even been in the same state. But if she'd never left him—if his shitty behavior hadn't forced her to reevaluate how she truly felt about his disability... Namely, she couldn't cope with it. Maybe she'd still be alive today. As would his every hope and dream for their shared future.

Now? He gazed out at the wondrous view and should have been awed. But all he really felt was empty. Afraid of never again feeling whole.

Even worse—he was terrified of going and doing something stupid like falling for Jane and her baby. Even if she didn't already have a man waiting for her, even if Gideon was in the right frame of mind to ponder a fresh start, it wouldn't matter.

The harsh reality was that even if he wanted Jane and her son to become an integral part of his life, Gideon knew deep down he would never be good enough.

Chapter Six

"You're safe. I was starting to worry." Jane had long since eaten her beef stroganoff and a Snickers. Chip had grown fitful, so she'd fed him again. When Gideon still hadn't returned and the darkness beyond the fire made her feel trapped in a too-small box, she'd grown angry. "But then I hoped a bear ate you."

"Fair enough." He joined her beside the fire.

"Is my company so bad that you prefer dark, scary woods?"

"Point of fact —" His gaze was too penetrating. Too direct. As if he couldn't just see who she was on the outside, but all the way into her soul. It unnerved her to the point that she wanted to look away, but couldn't. "I'm not afraid of the dark or whatever may or may not be lurking in the woods. What I am afraid of?"

He sighed.

While waiting for his answer, Jane's heart couldn't beat.

"Jane…" He laughed. "The truth is that I'm scared to death of you."

"Me?" Now she laughed. "That's the craziest thing I've ever heard."

"Then you're going to love this. Your baby makes me really nuts."

"Why?"

Head hanging, he wrung his hands. "The two of you remind me of what I used to have."

"You had a son?" She leaned in.

"No…" An endless pause was accentuated by the crackling fire "But my wife and I dreamed of having one—or four." His faint smile dissolved Jane's remaining anger, replacing it not with pity, but with sadness for whatever must have happened to tear his marriage apart.

"If you don't mind my asking, could your wife not have children?"

"No, no—nothing like that. Just bad timing. And then…" He stood, adding another log to the fire. "I botched certain situations very—"

"She didn't cheat on you, did she?"

"No." He shook his head vehemently. "She broke things off with me, but that's okay. In hindsight, she did the right thing."

"You're speaking of her in the past tense. Did she die?"

Crouching in front of the fire, he swallowed hard, and then nodded. Tears shone in his eyes.

"I'm so sorry. What happened?"

"You never let up, do you?"

"Occupational hazard." She faintly smiled. "Since I know nothing about myself, I guess that leaves me wanting to learn everything about you."

"Fair enough." He rose. Then paced. "A few years after our divorce, Missy was in a car accident. T-boned while passing through an intersection. I-I was told it happened fast—her death. She didn't suffer…"

The baby fussed.

Jane changed his position, but his cries grew louder.

"Is he hungry?" Gideon asked.

"No. I fed him right before you returned."

"Do you mind?" Approaching her, he held out his arms.

More than a little shocked, she asked, "You want to hold him?"

"As punishment for being late to base from weekend leave, I used to babysit for one of my superior officers—Tristan Bartoni. If I do say so myself, I was pretty good. His kids liked me so much, I started making decent money on the side whenever his wife needed shopping time."

Jane handed Gideon her son. During the exchange, their hands and forearms brushed. She shivered, but not due to being cold.

"Hey, little man…" Gideon spoke in a soft singsong voice that seemed to have Chip transfixed. Jane's heart swelled, while at the same time it ached. What could have happened to Gideon's marriage? "It may not be manly to describe you as beautiful, but damn…" He chuckled, tracing the baby's pale eyebrows with the tip of his pinky finger. "And what's up with this name your mom gave you? *Chip?* How are you going to be a big, strong fighter with a name like that?"

"You're going to be a lover, not a fighter—right, baby?" Jane stood, crossing to the two men currently filling her life.

"I can see that." There was a sad note to Gideon's voice. The baby fussed, wriggling against him. He froze for a few seconds, then held Chip out to her. "Take him."

She did, cradling her son close. But when that failed to calm him, she experimented with raising him to rest his cheek against her shoulder. Instinctively, she rocked while patting his back. Her efforts were rewarded with a shockingly loud burp for such a tiny body.

Jane gasped, then laughed.

Gideon joined in.

The tension that only moments earlier knotted between her shoulders now vanished.

"Did we just crack a top-secret parenting code?" she asked.

"You did." He cupped his big hand to the back of Chip's tiny head. The visual raised havoc in her stomach.

"Don't sell yourself short. If you hadn't returned him, I never would've tried the whole burping thing."

"Whatever. I'm just glad he stopped hurting."

"Me, too." For a moment, with dancing firelight banishing shadows and their mutual focus on the baby, they could have been a family on an ordinary campout. The notion was as heady as it was foolish. Gideon was not her baby's father. Yet in the moment, maybe she wanted him to be? It would have made her life so much simpler—knowing. The emotional vacuum wherein she currently resided was confusing and painful and downright depressing.

"Earlier?" He looked away, then said, "When I took off? I need to explain why—"

"Yes..." Why was her heart hammering? Why was it hard to breathe? What was she expecting?

"Nothing. It's not important." He shook his head. Her lungs deflated. She'd wanted—*needed*—his explanation for running away. Would he ever trust her enough to feel comfortable sharing? Granted, they hardly knew each other, but she wanted to know him. No longer knowing herself made her crave that intimacy. "What's for dinner? I'm starving."

"I already ate."

"You're too skinny. Eat again."

"What?" She wrinkled her nose, then laughed. "You're certifiable."

"Probably." He pushed back the tent flap, then ducked inside, presumably to forage for food. "What sounds good? Sweet-and-sour pork or chicken salad?"

"I'll take the pork."

"You would."

"What's that mean?"

He emerged from the tent carrying two freeze-dried food packets. "I *mean* that the only joy I have on this freakin' mountain is that pork, and now you're going to eat it."

"I'm sorry. You can have it."

"I'm messing with you." He stepped into the firelight's glow in time for her to catch him wink. "Eat up. You deserve it."

"What did I do?" Unprepared for Gideon pouring on his charm, she licked her lips before sucking in a few swift breaths.

"Gave birth in the woods? Less than twenty-four hours later, embarked on the kind of kick-ass hike that would have most soccer moms crying in less than an hour?" He filled the cast-iron pot with water from a gallon jug, then hung it over the fire. "And you figured out how to make your baby burp."

She waved off his compliments, but couldn't help but grin about her latest accomplishment. "You're right. That last feat for sure earned me a second dinner."

They ate and Jane coaxed Gideon into sharing a horse-training story about an Appaloosa named Marigold, who bit Gideon's behind so hard that he couldn't sit for a week. They discussed the logistics of returning to his cabin by early evening the next day. It would be a hard push, but doable.

"We should probably get some shut-eye," he said.

"Agreed. While you were gone, I rolled out your sleeping bag in the tent."

"Thanks, but given that growl you heard, I'll stay put here. Keep an eye on the fire."

"No way. We'll all be safer with you getting a decent night's rest. *Please.*"

He looked to the dazzling sky.

Without light pollution, the stars seemed close enough to touch. Their shimmer lent her an entire universe of hope.

By this time tomorrow, everything would change.

She would be reunited with family and friends and never see Gideon again. With Christmas only a few weeks away, as soon as she got home—wherever home was—she'd send him a fruit basket. That was the least she could do, considering all he'd done for her and her baby. No matter what her future entailed, she'd never forget his kindness or this special time they'd shared.

But for now? The thought of falling asleep without him beside her seemed impossible.

"Please," she quietly said, holding out her hand, "stay beside me. I can't explain why, I-I just don't want to be alone."

I know the feeling.

Gideon would never admit it to Jane, but he'd grown well acquainted with loneliness. Sometimes, the crushing weight of his solo existence grew more than he could bear. But he did. Not because he wanted to, but because he had no other choice.

Each bad decision that had led him to this place in time had been his own damned fault—right down to stepping on the land mine that had taken his leg. But curling up in a tent alongside Jane and her son? That didn't seem bad, but very, very good. Downright pleasant. By tomorrow they'd both be gone, but for now, nothing in the world sounded better than stretching out his weary body next to her—even if they had miles of down sleeping bags between them, that would be preferable to even one more night on his own.

Forcing a breath that he then held, he took her proffered hand and gave it a squeeze.

In tandem, they stood.

He reluctantly released her to bank the fire and unleash a slow, shaky exhale. Instead of her walking the short distance to the tent on her own, she hovered behind him, wreaking all manner of hormonal havoc. He felt her there. Might have just been his imagination, but he could have sworn that in his beating heart he felt the spark of her electrical energy. The shimmer of her radiant heat warmed his back.

Time slowed to the point that it seemed to take a week to finish the task, a year to find the strength to turn to face her. To pray she would never again hold out her hand. To ensure that the matter wasn't even an issue, he fished in his jeans pocket for an LED penlight, shining the way for Jane and her baby to safely enter the tent. He held back, giving her a moment to remove her shoes and shimmy into her bag.

Once she'd settled with a sigh, he entered.

He turned off his light, seeing by diffused moonlight and stars.

"You'd sleep better if you'd take off your boots."

"Thanks, Mom."

Keeping his boots on, he scrambled into his bag, thankful for the cover of patchy darkness.

"Thank you for sleeping with me."

"No problem." Only, considering the size of his erection, it was. Her words may have been innocent, but the bulge beneath his fly downright hurt.

"What animal do you really think made that growl?"

"Bigfoot."

"That doesn't make me feel better. This is the most bizarre thing to remember, but I have this vague recollection of a movie I once watched, and these people were out camping and he ate them one by one, and then—"

"Go to sleep. All that yammering attracts them."

For a blessed moment, she fell silent, but then, "Really? I thought they were just a myth?"

"Maybe?" In the darkness, a smile tickled his lips.

"No, be real."

Honey, he thought with an imaginary growl, *there's something big in this tent, but it sure as hell has nothing to do with my foot.*

JANE WOKE TO brilliant sun streaming through the open tent flap. The scent of fresh-brewed coffee and a touch of freeze-dried scrambled eggs with peppers made her stomach growl.

Squirrels chattered somewhere above the tent.

The stream gurgled.

"Hungry?" Gideon's sudden appearance startled her and Chip.

Hand to her chest, she said, "I will be once I recover from this heart attack."

"Sorry. The wind changed direction. That usually means we're in for a storm. If we're going to make it to my cabin by tonight, we should get this show on the road."

"You're right. But would you mind holding this little guy for a sec? I need to use the ladies' room."

"Um…" He glanced from her to the baby. "Sure. I can manage. But you'll hurry, right?"

She rolled her eyes before emerging from her sleeping bag to tug on her hiking boots, then take her biodegradable toilet paper from her pack.

It was a short trek to the trio of rocks where she had enough privacy to do her business. When she returned to camp, she got a shock to find her son naked and lying in the naturally formed bowl of a rock. Gideon had filled it with steaming water, and now dribbled it over the baby's downy hair, being careful not to get it in Chip's blue eyes.

The sight of this big, strong man tenderly caring for her son knotted her throat. Her eyes welled, and she hung back a moment to regain her composure. Tonight, she and her son might be back in their own home. But for now, this man and this natural cathedral were her home, and she never wanted to leave.

"Oh hey—hope you don't mind," Gideon said upon seeing her. "This kid was ripe."

"Tell me about it. What a great idea."

"Yesterday, I noticed this rock by the stream was holding water. I added the remains of the water I boiled for our breakfasts and voilà—we have a baby tub."

"I love it. Thank you."

"No problem." Was she imagining it, or was his smile extra broad? As if it made him feel good to help? "Want to take over?"

"Nope." She grinned. "Looks like you've got this situation under control, so I'm going to eat that breakfast you cooked. Oh—and I'm out of clean T-shirts to swaddle him in. Would you mind lending him one of yours?"

"Not a bit." He looked back to the baby, and his whole face softened. "Go ahead. I've got this."

"Thanks." She ate at her leisure, and while she could have enjoyed nature's panoramic view, it was more fun watching Gideon with her son. The man made the cutest chugging boat noises and though every baby book said newborns don't laugh or giggle or even smile, her baby looked awfully content, if not downright happy.

A coincidence? Or did he enjoy Gideon as much as she did?

Once Gideon finished Chip's bath, and even rigged up a more efficient paper towel diaper and snug T-shirt wrap, Jane fed him while Gideon broke down their camp.

They finished close to the same time, and then they were back on the trail, marching toward her uncertain future.

With each step, her hiking boots felt heavier— not because she was physically tired, but because she dreaded what was to come. Pure gut instinct told her there was no way she'd have been out in these woods so close to her due date without having been driven there—and she didn't mean by car. Someone was behind this, but who? Why? Who did she hate enough to have potentially risked her and her baby's lives?

Blue sky had long since been obliterated by gray. At this altitude, weather changed on a dime, and the temperature had already dropped twenty degrees. North wind lashed at her cheeks.

Chip was bundled to the point that only his nose and mouth were exposed.

"You look pale," Gideon said when they stopped for lunch in an alpine meadow.

"I feel pale." She dropped to her knees on a grassy sea, laying Chip beside her. "How much farther?"

"We're not making great time. I'm guessing we have at least ten miles to go."

She groaned.

"Unless…" He set down her pack, repositioning his saddlebags to allow access to a side pocket. He withdrew a cell phone and turned it on. "I'll be damned. I've got a bar."

"Who are you calling?"

"Nine-one-one. You and the baby need to get out of here. From the looks of it, by morning, this meadow will be buried in snow."

"What about you?"

He shrugged.

The faint sound of ringing carried on the wind.

"Gideon," she said, "you can't—"

A woman picked up. "Nine-one-one, please state your emergency…"

Thirty minutes later, wind whipped from the force of an approaching chopper's rotors. The temperature had dropped another twenty degrees. Light snow was already falling.

"This is wild," she said. "I can't believe we're about to be rescued. I'm scared about my memory returning, but I'm craving hot chocolate more. What are you looking forward to getting back to?"

"Look," he said, "this is where I'm getting off this ride. I need to get back to my animals. I never planned on staying out this long."

"What do you mean?" She searched his face for signs she'd heard him wrong.

"You know exactly what I mean. I promised to keep you and the rug rat safe, and now that I'm done…"

That knot in her throat grew to the size of a peach.

Just like that? He was walking away from her and Chip? Hadn't their time together meant anything?

Of course not. Was she mental? A wave of nausea rushed through her. What she'd taken as a meaningful friendship—a relationship—he'd seen as just him helping a stranger. He'd told her as much. Only she was too weak-minded to have truly listened.

The helicopter hovered above them before dropping. The ground shook. Cold wind sliced through her, but it felt downright balmy compared to the chill emanating from Gideon.

Was this really how he wanted their last moments together to be? Not even a friendly goodbye?

The aircraft's side doors opened and a pair of EMTs hopped out, then ran toward her. "Ma'am? Are you able to walk?"

"Y-yes." Her teeth chattered. She held her baby extra close, shielding him from the wind.

"This way…" The man approaching her was a human mountain. He sported a full beard and gentle smile, wrapping her in a thick wool blanket, then helping her and Chip toward the waiting chopper. There was so much she needed and wanted to say to Gideon, but what was the use? He wouldn't even make eye contact, so why should she waste her breath shouting above the chopper's noise?

Clearly, as he handed her pack to the other EMT, Gideon was as glad to be rid of her as she was terrified to go. What did that say about her? What was wrong with her to have fallen so hard, so fast for a man when she didn't know her own name? It wasn't just sad, but pathetic.

But she had a son to raise. For him, she needed to be a strong.

She and Chip were helped aboard the helicopter, and the pilot lifted them into the glowering sky. As abruptly as Gideon had entered her life, he was gone.

A memory. A ghost.

Jane was well and truly on her own.

Chapter Seven

Gideon shielded his eyes from dust and blowing snow.

He should have looked away from the chopper, but couldn't.

At some point while bathing Jane's son, he'd changed his mind. He'd wanted the baby and his mother to himself a while longer. But then the weather had changed, and he'd known even Mother Nature thought his forging a deeper bond with them was a bad idea.

He'd put on a show for Jane, making her believe he was randomly checking his cell signal, when all along, he'd banked on this being her exit point.

Had he flown with them, not only would he have been stuck at the hospital with no vehicle, damn near fifty miles from his cabin, but he would have had to watch Jane's rightful family claim her.

When all traces of Jane and her son faded until the only sound remaining was wind howling through the pines, Gideon settled his cowboy hat lower on his forehead, raised his coat's collar, then started walking. Minus Jane's pack, with only his saddlebags slung over his shoulder, his pace tripled.

He'd been blessed with a state-of-the-art prosthetic limb—a carbon fiber socket with a plastic molded foot designed to fit into his favorite pair of cowboy boots.

For the most part, it felt good, but it hadn't been designed for walking long distances or trudging over rocky terrain. Most of his work was done either in the paddock or on a horse's back. The strain of the past couple days wore on him in a dull throb that he used his past SEAL training to ignore.

Just as if he were on a mission, he didn't have the luxury of quitting.

By twilight, he rounded the last corner of the trail.

Six inches of snow had fallen, and never was he happier to see his stone cabin. But then it dawned on him that light shone golden through the front window panes. Smoke spiraled up from the chimney.

He had company. No doubt, Mrs. Gentry.

He should have been glad for the company, the heat and the possibility of a decent meal waiting inside, but the only emotion he could muster was frustration.

Why did I let them go?

He squelched the ridiculous thought in favor of ducking into the barn. Sure enough, there stood Jelly Bean, looking mighty proud of herself in her stall. Mrs. Gentry must have filled her water and feed.

The horse neighed.

"Don't play nice after the trouble you caused." Despite his harsh words, he rubbed her cheek.

She whinnied, bobbing her head in appreciation.

If it hadn't been for Jelly Bean's disappearing act, Gideon wouldn't have been forced into spending two days and nights with Jane and her son. He wouldn't be second-guessing everything from putting her on that chopper without him to sharing her tent to holding her hand. He wouldn't be consumed with questions over what she was doing. Who was she with?

Gideon's every primal urge told him to punch the

nearest wall, but if he did that, he'd spook the damned horse who was to blame for all of his troubles in the first place.

"Thinking about her?"

"What?" Startled, Gideon looked up to find all four feet ten inches of Mrs. Hildegarde Gentry. She wore her long white hair in a single braid down her back and sported a turquoise fringed poncho, hot-pink rain boots and a yellow beanie hat she'd probably made for herself. Her husband had long since died of cancer, but she had six kids and eight grandkids, all of whom lived close enough that they should have been keeping a closer watch on her, so she wasn't constantly bugging him.

"I heard all about that woman you rescued on my police scanner. That's some kind of excitement. Everyone's talking."

"Thanks for looking after Jelly Bean. Are my chickens and the donkey okay?"

"Your whole crew is fine. Now tell me everything. Did you really help deliver her baby?"

He scratched his head. It was a damned shame that the rumor mill on this mountain couldn't be put to better use—like grinding flour instead of gossip.

"Kyle Fletcher down at the feed store said you had to fend off a mountain lion from eating the poor baby? And the itty-bitty thing is four months premature? And the only thing it would eat was the broth from freeze-dried meals?"

"Are you tipsy on your homemade blackberry wine?"

"You'd better watch your sassy mouth, Gideon Snow. You're not too old for a good old-fashioned belt whupping."

"Yes, ma'am." He opened the sliding barn door, gesturing for her to lead the way.

She exited into driving snow. "You can't blame me for being curious—or the rest of the folks up here."

"All three of you?" He left the barn and closed the door.

Aside from current company, his neighbors consisted of eccentric old Igor Ivanov and his equally nutty cousin, Peter. They worked a gold claim from which no one had ever seen a speck of gold. That said, they drove a brand-new Range Rover and per Mrs. Gentry had filled their dilapidated RV with a vast array of technical gadgetry.

"There you go, being sassy again!" The wind had picked up. Near whiteout conditions made it tough to find the cabin's front door. At least the wind's lonely howl somewhat drowned out Mrs. Gentry.

Gideon beat her to the stairs, then held her arm to steady her on the way up.

"Let me go. I'm not an invalid!"

"Duly noted." She didn't mount the slightest sign of struggle until reaching the covered porch, then she yanked her arm free.

She'd parked her four-wheeler close enough to his pickup that he was guessing she'd hit it, then backed up to hide the damage. It wouldn't be the first time.

Come morning, he'd look for a fresh dent and send her a bill.

He opened the cabin's door and damn near moaned with pleasure from the heat. His cheeks and nose stung.

"You're an idiot for not hitching a ride in the chopper."

"True." He removed his coat, hat and gloves, hanging them all on a rack by the door. "And when are you leaving?"

She snorted on her way to the kitchen.

The three-room stone cabin consisted of one main room where he did most of his living, a utility closet, the bedroom and a bath. The place had been built back in the twenties, supposedly as a stopover for liquor runners during Prohibition.

He'd bought the cabin and fifty acres for a ridiculously cheap price—then he'd started renovations and discovered he hadn't gotten such a bargain after all. Gideon added a new roof and gutted the bath and kitchen—adding all new fixtures and appliances, as well as a roomy tub.

Might not be his most manly trait, but since losing his leg, he enjoyed a good, long soak in steaming water—in the dark, because it made him physically ill looking at his stump.

"Judging by the snow," she said, "I'll be staying the night. I did work for my lodging, though. You have clean sheets and that heavenly smell is my world-famous beef stew and fresh-baked bread. I meant to go out and get you a Christmas tree, but ran out of daylight."

"Thanks for the food, but the last thing I want is a Christmas tree." He stomped the snow from his boots, then strode to the fire to warm his stinging hands.

"Whyever not? I was thinking that maybe once Jane and her baby leave the hospital—assuming her family still hasn't claimed her—you might have her over for a visit. I could whip up a meal, invite a few neighbors. We'll have a party."

"Please, stop." He pressed his fingers to his forehead. "With any luck, Jane and her son are back with their family and I'll never see them again. End of story."

"Something tells me it's not quite that simple." She removed two bowls from the cabinet to the right of the sink, then filled them with stew. His mouth watered and stomach growled. "Would you mind pouring me a nice glass of milk?"

"Don't have any."

"Sure you do. I brought it along with the stew fixings."

Of course you did. He got her milk, a beer for himself, then met her at the table.

It wasn't his intention to be rude, but he'd finished his bowl before Mrs. Gentry made a dent in hers. Then Gideon realized he hadn't even waited for her to say grace—which was her usual fee for a meal.

"Sorry about skipping your blessing. Guess I worked up an appetite during the last of my hike."

"I'm sure the Lord will take that into consideration. Would you like more?"

"Yes, ma'am. But I'll get it myself."

He'd had thirds before she finished her first.

Outside, the wind howled and rattled the windows, but the stone walls didn't budge.

"You've got a nice, solid place here," Mrs. Gentry noted. "Any woman would be thrilled to marry you—not Jane. She's probably taken. But some lucky lady. Just sayin'."

Gideon groaned.

Finally full, he pushed back his bowl and stretched out his legs under the table. He sighed. It wasn't any *lucky lady* who popped into his mind's eye, but Jane. How were she and Chip doing?

"You're thinking of her, aren't you? Your mystery gal?"

Yes, damn it. "No."

"You're entitled, you know? To think about a woman. Not necessarily this one, since she's no doubt spoken for. But you know what I mean."

"Entitled to what?"

"Happiness. I know after your wife died—"

"Missy wasn't my wife anymore. We were divorced."

"Semantics. Any fool could tell you still carried a torch. All I'm saying is—"

"It's late, and I've had a couple of shitty days. How about we table this topic?"

"Only under one condition."

"Name it."

"You do the dishes and I get the bed."

Gideon sighed. "Remind me why I gave you a key to my place?"

"Because I feed your livestock for free and make a mean pot of stew? Oh—and I'm the closest thing to a mother you've got."

"You fight as dirty as any man I've known." He'd already started filling the sink with hot water.

"Thank you. If you need me, I'll be in the restroom, putting on my night creams."

She was a good woman—drove him nuts, but he really did think of her as a mom. His own mom had a heart attack a few years back—not that they'd ever been close. She'd run off with a biker when Gideon was six or seven. His dad raised him, but he'd died of chronic obstructive pulmonary disease not long after Gideon's eighteenth birthday. Having no family had made him that much more determined to form his own, but look how disastrous that had turned out.

Another reason it was a good thing Jane was now safely back with her family.

He scooped leftover stew into one of the Tupperware bowls Mrs. Gentry had long ago gifted him, then snapped on the lid. He wrapped the remaining bread in foil. She was a great cook, but needed to add more sweets to her repertoire.

Once the kitchen was clean, Gideon added two logs to the fire, put the metal grate firmly in place, then grabbed an extra blanket and pillow from the utility closet. He never used to have extras until Mrs. Gentry brought them. She was an odd duck, but she was the sole person standing between him and talking to only his horse clientele and the donkey and chickens.

Even through his closed bedroom door, his guest could be heard snoring.

Gideon had just tossed his bedding on the sofa when he heard an engine. Headlights shone through the front windows.

Who in their right mind would be out in this storm?

He peered beyond the plaid curtains Mrs. Gentry made to get a shock. The sheriff exited his SUV, then trudged through the snow and up the stairs. Gideon had known West Moorefield since basic. In fact, West had been the one who'd told him about the cabin going up for auction.

Gideon flung open the door. "Get in here, man!"

"Thanks." West dusted the snow from his hat and shoulders before stepping inside. "That is some brutal wind." He shrugged free of his heavy coat.

"Not that I don't enjoy shooting the shit with you, but you sure could've picked a better night to visit."

"Tell me about it." He kicked off his boots to go stand by the fire.

"So why did you drive all the way out here?"

Gideon's old friend furrowed his brow. He hesitated, as if searching for the right words. Then he forced a deep breath.

"Out with it. You're spooking me." In another time, given a situation like this, Gideon would have been scared for a member of his family. But since he had no family... *Jane*. Her pretty features flashed before him. Could something be wrong with Jane?

"Sorry. No cause for alarm—at least, I don't think so. But remember that Jane Doe you called about?"

Gideon's pulse took off at a hard canter.

JANE TOSSED AND turned in the too-narrow hospital bed. It was far wider than her sleeping bag, so why had she felt more comfortable there? Because Gideon had been beside her. What she wouldn't give to talk to him.

Upon reaching the hospital, time felt as if it were moving in fast-forward. She'd been poked and prodded and worst of all, Chip had been taken to the nursery where they'd done a fancier job of cutting his cord, then discovered he had jaundice. He was now receiving phototherapy, but that meant he was allowed to be with her only when he was feeding. Worst of all, the family she'd anticipated would be waiting for her? Didn't exist. No one came.

Upon learning no one wanted her, she'd burst into an embarrassing round of sobs that had stopped only under medicinal sedation. Long story short? She'd suffered a good old-fashioned nervous breakdown.

Now it was the middle of the night.

Beyond a picture window that ran the room's length, snow blew nearly horizontal beneath the eerie orange glow of the parking lot lights.

All she could think about was Gideon. Had he made it safely to his cabin? Had Jelly Bean been waiting? Though he was a stranger, her time spent with him seemed more real than her current situation. What happened if authorities never found her family? Was there such a thing as orphanages for adults?

"Still awake?" A nurse bustled into her room.

"Unfortunately. Has anyone asked about me?"

"I'm sorry, sweetie, but no." After checking IV fluid levels, she took Jane's vitals. "Want me to ask your doctor if it's all right for you to have meds to help you sleep?"

"That would be great. Thanks."

Once again on her own, Jane closed her eyes, trying to relax, but she couldn't stop reviewing her official diagnosis.

A doctor with a shock of red hair, blue glasses, faded jeans and a Walking Dead T-shirt had said, "Judging by the bruise on your forehead, you have traumatic amnesia. Given time, your full memory should return. With plenty of rest and trying not to stress about it, I'll bet by Christmas your memories will return along with your family."

Right. And if she were really lucky, maybe Santa would bring her a pair of blue Converse high-tops just like his.

Jane was trying not to be bitter or angry or downright freaked out, but how was she supposed to even pay her hospital bill? She had no money, no ID—hardly any personal possessions at all save for her camping gear and a backpack loaded with clothes so ripe she smelled them from the bed.

Her heart beat loud enough for her to hear in her ears. Panic raised bile in the back of her throat.

What was she going to do? Upon her release, how would she care for herself? Let alone her baby?

A knock sounded on her room door. Expecting

the nurse with medicine, Jane said, "Thank goodness you're—"

When she saw who really stood in the open door, a fresh onslaught of tears stole her ability to speak.

Chapter Eight

"It's you…"

"In the flesh…" Nerves made Gideon wink. *Wink?* What the hell was he thinking? He wasn't. The whole ride to the hospital, Gideon had been frozen with fear. What if Jane forgot him? What if something serious happened to Chip? Irrational—ridiculous—scenarios swirled round and round his head, dropping faster than the snow. But now he was with her again, and all he could think was that she was bound to be trouble.

"I never thought I'd see you again." The room's faint light accentuated silent tears glistening on her cheeks.

"Ditto. Lucky for you, I have friends in high places. The sheriff told me you might need a place to stay?"

A hiccoughed sob escaped her. She removed a half dozen tissues from a box, wadding them to her face. How could she breathe under all that paper?

"Is that a yes or no?" In their time in the woods, she'd done her fair share of crying, but this was different. This was raw, ragged emotion.

Apparently unable to speak, she nodded.

He should go to her.

Hug her and whisper kind words into her freshly washed hair. But to do that would invite her further into his carefully structured world. Forcing himself not to touch her, he rammed his hands in his jeans pocket.

"I, ah, heard your little man is sick, but he's going to be okay?"

The question earned him another nod.

"That's good. Real good." Spying an uncomfortable-looking straight-backed chair, he dragged it to her bedside, then had a seat. Something about her pale complexion, tear-dampened cheeks and pained expression had a wave of tenderness washing over him. But also a sense of duty.

He'd found this woman and her child, and until her family stepped forward, he'd do right by her. There. That was the perfect solution to the fact that he couldn't allow himself to be with her, but wanted to.

Duty had to be honored. He'd taken vows.

You're not fooling anyone, man.

He hated that nagging voice of reason.

Your Navy days are far behind you. If you bring this woman and her child into your home, it's for one reason only—because you're sick and tired of being alone. And Mrs. Gentry's company doesn't count.

His palms grew clammy. Air had become a rare commodity.

"Thank you," Jane said. "I promise not to be a bother. I'll cook and keep things tidy and—"

"Whoa." Gideon held up his hands. "This is a strictly temporary gig, and you're sure not coming to be my serving wench, but to rest."

She laughed through more tears. "Got it."

"So Chip is going to be okay?" Gideon had to be sure.

"Jaundice is common in preemies. They're keeping him under a special light, but he won't need it for much longer."

"Good. Are you okay?"

"Sort of." She forced another smile, but this one didn't reach her eyes. Green eyes that for some odd reason reminded him of Christmas cookie sprinkles. "The doctor said that physically, I check out fine, and that the kind of memory loss I have usually doesn't last long."

"That's a good thing, right?"

"Well, sure, but in the meantime, where does that leave me? I have nowhere to live, no money, no job— not even a valid form of ID. I'm a ghost. And Christmas is coming. Poor little Chip won't even have a proper C-Christmas tree."

"Shh…" Gideon's conscience couldn't take one more round of tears. He rose from his seat to deliver an awkward hug that was more of a sideways pat that left him wanting to crawl into bed alongside her, holding her close until her every fear and tear subsided. "As soon as you're released, we're going to grab all the baby gear you need, and then you can help me turn my cabin into the North Pole, okay?"

Caution alarms clanged in Gideon's head and heart, warning him to turn back now. *Danger ahead!* All his honor had promised this woman and her baby were food and shelter. What the hell made him think he was emotionally strong enough to deal with a big holiday and all the trappings? Especially when at any minute, Jane's family could show.

This situation was growing into the equivalent of an emotional suicide bomb. He was inviting his own heart to get not just hurt, but annihilated.

Yet all for the low, low price of seeing Jane's fragile smile, of smelling the clean, soapy scent of her hair, he didn't care.

BY THE NEXT AFTERNOON, the sun was shining and Jane had been released from Pine Glade Memorial. Chip had to stay an additional day for more light treatments.

Gideon had been busy—getting a ride home from his friend, West, washing her clothes so she'd have a clean outfit to wear shopping, then returning to town to book two rooms at a local inn.

She now sat at the foot of her room's bed, mind reeling from how fast all of this had transpired. Gideon operated with military precision. He'd made lists for everything—baby supplies, toiletries, healthy foods for breastfeeding moms. The sheer number of items to be bought made her dizzy. And the cost? She'd keep all receipts, reimbursing him to the last penny.

The Shamrock Inn had been built in 1910 with a charming Victorian exterior. Her room had a sun-flooded bay window housing a small antique table and chairs. The brass bed was covered with a pale blue wedding ring–patterned quilt. Blue-striped wallpaper rose from glowing hardwood floors that were original to the building. Frilly white curtains and fluffy area rugs added an extra feminine touch to the room that a brass plaque labeled the Bonnie Blue Suite. Tiffany lamps and a blue velvet upholstered settee completed the historical feel. A silver foil Christmas tree twinkled with blue lights and dozens of sparkly blue vintage glass ornaments.

Thankfully, a modern bathroom had been added.

The suite would make the perfect romantic getaway. She'd like to believe herself madly in love with her baby's father, but her gut told her that wasn't the case. Why would she have run from someone she adored? It didn't make sense.

A knock sounded at the adjoining door between her and Gideon's rooms. "Ready?" he asked, his voice muffled.

She opened the door. "Yes, but I want you to know I'm paying you back—for everything. Even this room. I'm guessing it cost a small fortune."

"Not necessary."

"It's very necessary. I don't want to be a burden."

"Then you should've stayed home instead of going hiking when you were about to pop out your baby."

"That's not nice. I'm sure I had a very good reason for being out in those woods."

"I'm sure you did, but until we learn what that reason was, I'm going to continue giving you grief. I mean, if you think about it, it is kind of funny, right?"

She fixed him with a hard stare.

He held up his hands in surrender. "Okay, maybe not so funny. Sorry. I'm trying to make light of a rough situation."

"Don't." Before leaving the room, she felt the urge to grab her purse, but then remembered that even if she had one, there was no wallet or lipstick or gum to put in it.

"I know this pout," Gideon said upon opening the room's outer door. "What's wrong?"

"I-I hate feeling so...*naked*."

He reddened. "Trust me, you're fully clothed."

"I meant in a deeper sense. I was instinctively going to grab my purse, but I don't have one. Since I have no belongings, I don't have need for one. It's unsettling."

"We'll add a purse to our list."

"You don't get it. I want to know who I am. I presumably have a lifetime of memories and photos. Family and friends. Where are they? Where is my stuff? I feel as if I got dropped on that mountain by aliens."

"You need to chill." Gideon closed the door. He planted his big hands on her shoulders, then propelled her backward until she was sitting on the edge of the bed. "Neither of us have a crystal ball to see into your past or future, which leaves us with limited choices. A—your family shows up. B—your memory makes a sudden comeback. C—we try making the best of this situation by ensuring you're as comfortable and happy as possible in the time we have together."

"You made that sound as if I'm dying."

"You know what I mean." He took a chair from the table in front of the bay window and sat to face her. "To a certain extent, Jane, as we knew her—*you*—will be gone as soon as you remember your identity. Until then, aside from working with Jelly Bean, my schedule is wide open. My neighbor, Mrs. Gentry, is watching my chickens and donkey and the horse, and is beside herself with excitement over the prospect of meeting you. Christmas is right around the corner, and though I'm not big on holidays, since this is Chip's first one, let's do it up right. While we're in town, we'll grab lights—"

"Can we make all the ornaments?"

"Why not? Just add what supplies you need to our list."

She laughed. "That list of yours is going to rival Santa's."

"True." He reached for her, hovering his hands midway between them.

Please touch me, hold me, her heart begged. More than she needed any random item on his list, she craved human contact—his contact. But was that wrong? For all she knew, she could be married. Did that make her an awful person? *Yes*.

Hands clamped firmly on her knees, Jane licked her lips.

Gideon also held his hands to his knees, and for the longest time their gazes locked.

Her senses dulled; all ambient noise faded until her sole focus was Gideon's lips and how badly she wanted his arms wrapped around her, with him whispering sweet reassurances in her ear, sweeping kisses down her jaw and chin and then finally, deliciously, her…

She gulped enough air to make her cough.

"You okay?" he asked, standing to pat her back. She'd craved feeling his touch, but not like this.

"I'm fine." She waved off his concern. "Let's go. And I want detailed receipts for every penny you spend."

"Yes, ma'am."

PINE GLADE WAS too small for a Walmart or Target, but they did have Kingman's General Store and Lumber Yard that carried just about any item anyone could ever need—a good thing considering that aside from camping gear, Jane and Chip were starting from scratch.

"Do you want to find baby stuff first?" Gideon asked while grabbing a big green cart. "Or mommy stuff?"

"Baby," she said with a firm nod. "But I like being called Mommy. It has a nice ring."

"Wait until you get your first college tuition bill or a late-night police call." Gideon rolled the cart toward a tower of diapers.

"My son is going to be a rocket scientist and win lots of scholarships, plus the Nobel Prize."

"I'll be honored to say I knew him when he wore these." Gideon tossed two packs of extra-small Huggies and a box of wipes into the cart. It would be a relief to no longer use paper towels. "What else does the little man need?"

"Baby shampoo." She took a golden bottle from the shelf. "For sure, lotion."

"This." Gideon added a purple floating dinosaur.

"Gideon, no. I'm on a tight budget."

"How do you know? Maybe you're an heiress?" He tossed in two teething rings, a bath seat, a bath basin, and a T. rex hooded towel. "Just in case, don't you think he should be prepared?"

"For first-class bathing?" She cracked a smile, and Gideon liked it. Too much. Just like he was enjoying shopping for her son, he liked teasing Jane. Even if her family never showed up, that didn't mean he would ever be able to claim her for himself. He was broken. No number of smiles in the world could fix that.

But they sure went a long way toward making me feel better. As if life is worth living.

He tabled those rogue thoughts in favor of taking a good-looking wicker bassinet from a top shelf. "What do you think? Something portable like this? Or would you prefer a standard crib?"

"I like it."

"Done." He took contents of the cart out to instead place them in the bassinet, then put the larger item in the cart. "We need baby sheets and blankets. What about a mobile?"

"How would we attach it to the bassinet?"

"Good point." By the time they'd finished in the baby aisles, the cart was heaped higher than Jane's head. They added a car seat and stroller, then cautiously wound their way toward the checkout.

"I will repay you for every bit of this," Jane said under her breath at the checkout.

"Not necessary."

"Not up for debate."

Gideon wasn't surprised when the bill added up to well over a thousand dollars, but that was okay. His expenses were minimal, and he had more than enough in savings to cover the occasional splurge.

"What am I going to do?" Jane asked on their way to the truck. "That cost a fortune. No way am I now going to turn around and have you buy items for me, too."

"Fair enough. You sit in the truck and guard everything in the bed." While she stood with her hands on her hips, glaring, Gideon started to unload.

"That's not what I meant, and you know it." She covered a yawn. "Please, don't buy anything more. This is already embarrassing enough."

"What kind of woman are you? Here I am, offering to spring for a major shopping spree for not only your son, but you, and all you've done the whole time is complain. How about showing a little gratitude?"

"Thank you."

"That's it?" he teased. "Not even a hug?"

Before Gideon had time to think through his hasty request, she bolted forward and wrapped her arms around him, unwittingly mounding her full breasts against his abs. Until now, he hadn't realized how tiny she was. How perfectly she fit against him. His chin rested atop her smooth dark hair. She smelled so good. Clean and pure. She hadn't been soiled by life like him.

When she released him, it took every ounce of willpower not to draw her back in.

Her eyes filled with tears, but her perfect bow-shaped lips smiled. "I really do appreciate all you're doing. No one has ever been this nice."

"How do you know?" he asked.

"I guess I don't. But I feel it. You're a good man, Gideon Snow."

If only that were true. What Jane didn't know—must

never know—was that his heart was black. Filled with tar and soot and rage.

Since losing his leg, he was incapable of true good.

This foray into "Happyland" didn't count.

What did? Making sure he never lost sight of the fact that however much he craved normalcy or Jane and Chip's combined light, he didn't deserve either. He didn't deserve anything other than more endless, empty days contemplating how badly he'd hurt Missy. He needed to remember his vow to never hurt a woman again—even if it had been unintentionally.

Chapter Nine

Jane looked at herself in the dressing room mirror and fought a sudden flood of panic. Her heart raced. Fingers and toes went numb. A woman stared back at her, but Jane couldn't recall having ever seen her before.

Without trying on the jeans and sweater Gideon had picked for her, she burst out of the dressing room, hurling herself against him. "I don't want to try on clothes."

"Why?" he asked. "What's wrong? You're trembling."

She clung to him. *Never let me go.*

"Hey…" Hands on her shoulders, he gently nudged her far enough back for him to meet her wide-eyed gaze. "What happened in there?"

"I-I don't know," she said. "I guess I fully saw myself in the mirror for the first time since losing my memory and realized I've never seen this woman. I must sound like a lunatic—I mean, I somehow know it's me, but I don't remember me. It's terrifying. Please get me out of here. I just want to hold my baby and be with you."

"Sure." He handed her his truck keys. They'd locked their previous purchases in the cab. "Go on outside. I'll pay for the stuff we already have in the cart."

"No. I don't want it."

"Jane—come on. You need the toothbrush. The shampoo and soap and other *lady* items." He reddened.

"Okay…" As much as she hated to admit it, he was right. "But please hurry."

She gripped the keys tightly enough that they bit her palm.

Outside, the sun shone and the temperature was in the fifties. With no wind, the day felt downright balmy. Mounded snow piles rapidly melted, sounding like a babbling stream while cascading into sewage drains. She breathed deeply of the conifer-laced air. The mountain town had been carved out of the forest. A chatty nurse had told her the main industry used to be logging, but was now tourism. Looking up and down the bustling street, it was easy to see why.

The storefronts resembled a thriving Old West town, with wide wooden boardwalks. Balconies jutted out from second stories. She imagined saloon girls hanging over the spindled rails, shouting at passersby to brag about their services.

Reminders of the approaching holiday included giant candy canes strapped to old-fashioned black lampposts and pine garland draped from railings and windowsills, festooned with red bows. "Jingle Bells" played over a sound system, and antsy children hopped and whined while waiting to see Santa, who reigned over the toy workshop set up in a small park nestled between a toy store and a day spa.

A flyer on the toy store window advertised a church spaghetti supper. The date was for tonight—she knew, because it was the same as her hospital discharge papers.

How wonderful would it be to raise a family in this idyllic place? To meet with friends at long church tables, couples laughing and sharing stories while their children played.

Rooting herself in her immediate surroundings calmed her, as did dreaming of hopefully not-too-far-off better days.

After forcing several deep breaths, she felt more herself—whoever that may be.

While Gideon was inside, she'd lost count of how many times the street's lone stoplight turned. A steady stream of cars moved through.

He finally emerged carrying five bulging bags—far more stuff than she recalled being in their cart.

"Where did you get all of that?" she asked.

"I needed a few things, too."

That made sense. She was relieved he hadn't bought more for her or Chip. He'd already done enough. With no job, she wasn't sure how she'd pay him back.

Together, they unloaded previous purchases into the truck's bed, then set off for the hospital.

The cramped space had grown warm. Hershey's bar and Twinkie wrappers littered the floor. The sun had baked them, creating enough of a sugary scent to make her stomach growl.

"Hungry?" Gideon asked.

"I am now. When you said you like sweets, I thought you'd been joking, but you have a serious addiction—I like it." She laughed.

"Guilty." He reached past her to open the glove box, in the process brushing the knees of her jogging pants. Warm tingles radiated from the epicenter of his touch. Candy and individually wrapped baked goods avalanched onto her feet.

"Gideon!" She couldn't stop staring—and laughing. "Are you running an illegal candy cartel?"

"Wouldn't you like to know." After a dashing wink, he leaned deep into her personal space, plucking goodies from the floor to set them in the center of the bench seat.

Lord, he looks and smells good... She needed to fan herself from his heat, but didn't dare move for fear of embarrassing herself by reaching out to him, drawing him even closer. She'd already made enough of a spectacle in the store. For once, she needed to keep her cool.

Up close and personal, his size dwarfed her. Made her feel delicate. Protected.

Finished with his task, he grinned, gesturing to his haul. "Eat up. That's lunch."

"I'm eating for two," she blurted. "Chip needs something more substantial than a Snickers."

"Damn. I was afraid you'd say that. How about we share one to hold us over till we're done with our hospital visit?"

"Perfect." They decided to open a two-pack of chocolate cupcakes. While hers was delicious, the best part wasn't the taste, but watching Gideon enjoy his. He closed his eyes while chewing, and his lips curved into a dreamy smile.

The man did enjoy his sweets.

And I enjoy him...

AT THE HOSPITAL, while Jane breastfed her son, Gideon roamed the halls, searching for anything to clear his mind of the image of her laughing in his truck, or hugging him when she'd feared her own reflection. The fact that she truly needed him in so many varied ways had never been more evident. Sadly, the fact that he thrived on the feeling of *being* needed was also apparent.

What was he going to do?

He wouldn't even try denying that for the moment, playing house was proving fun, but it wouldn't last. Sooner or later her family would show. Even if they didn't, his physical shortcomings forced him to push her away.

What woman in her right mind would want to be intimate with a man missing half of his leg?

I'm sorry! Missy had cried the last time they'd tried making love. *I'm just not attracted to you. I tried telling myself your losing part of your leg didn't matter, but it does. I tried being polite, but the stump—it disgusts me.*

Jaw tight, fists clenched, Gideon struggled to escape the nightmarish scene. Times like these, he envied Jane's lack of memory. She had no idea what a blessing it was.

"Whoa—what's got you in such a hurry?" West stood at the ER's reception desk, filling out a form.

"Oh—hey, man. I was, ah, just going for some air."

"Hold up. I'll join you."

Swell. The last thing Gideon needed was company.

West signed the bottom of a few pages, then waved his hand for Gideon to follow him out of the chaotic waiting area to an outside courtyard.

Snow had been shoveled into giant piles that were now melting into sloppy gray puddles. Two little kids shrieked in a snowball fight while a nearby woman he assumed to be their mom smoked a cigarette and talked on her phone.

West headed for a concrete bench and sat.

Gideon followed. The surface was cold, biting through the ass and legs of his jeans. It was good. It reminded him that he was alive and Missy was dead and Jane and her cherubic son were only temporary fixtures in his messed-up life.

"One of Jane Doe's nurses told me you got her a room while her kiddo is still stuck in here. You're a good guy, you know?"

Gideon shrugged off the compliment. "Anyone would have done the same."

"Nah. Not the jackholes I deal with. I just brought in a kid who—" He winced. "Never mind. I'd rather talk about anything but him. So back at the station, I ran a missing persons check, but came up empty. It's the damnedest thing."

"Tell me about it. I felt sure she'd have family waiting for her once she got to town."

"I'm not giving up. I talked with Lyle Hatterous— he's a park ranger over the entire Asuaguih region. He said that the recent snows made a couple of possible trail entrances impassable. At that elevation, nothing's thawed, but as soon as he can get a man in there, he'll check lots for abandoned cars. He did warn that with manpower being cut, it could be a while—at least until after the holidays. Are you all right to keep her till then?"

"Yeah. I'm good." Gideon downplayed his true emotions. God help him, but the news made him downright giddy. That was wrong.

"You're awesome. Thanks. Seriously, you restore my faith in humanity."

"Stop. It's not a big deal."

"It is. And if I were on speaking terms with our lady mayor, I'd nominate you for a medal." West laughed. The mayor also happened to be West's wife. They must have squabbled over their Cheerios.

The radio West wore on his hip squawked. "Sheriff, Crawly brothers are at it again. Paul is still held up at that accident scene on Rose and Lilac. Think you can head over before they kill each other?"

"Will do, Carla. Over and out." He shook his head and sighed. "What'd I tell you? Don't these fools know it's almost Christmas? It's been great talking with you, man. I'll let you know as soon as I hear word about Jane."

West jogged toward his SUV, which Gideon only just noticed had been parked in a space reserved for an ambulance. A fire truck was parked in the space reserved for the sheriff. It would be funny if the situation Gideon found himself in weren't so confusing.

What was wrong with him? Actually anticipating sharing a holiday with a woman and child who were essentially on loan. He was messed up. But then Missy had been all too happy to tell him so right up until the end.

He ducked back through automatic doors.

The ER was a nightmare he was glad to leave behind. Too much coughing and moaning and families sniping back and forth for his liking.

He wound his way through the maze of halls that was surprising for a small regional hospital, but eventually landed back in the maternity ward. The walls were pink near the elevators, but blue in the waiting area. Christmas had exploded in red foil garland. Paper gift and elf cutouts had been taped to the walls.

Two babies slept in plastic bassinets behind the nursery proper's glass walls. He caught sight of Jane feeding her son. Her expression was one of pure bliss. He wanted to avert his gaze—should have—but physically couldn't.

If he hadn't lost his leg, this might have been his life with Missy. But plenty of guys he'd served with had not only lost limbs, but learned to live with chronic pain. They soldiered on. They had wives and kids and dogs. They were normal. Why was he the only one struggling with the fact that his disfigurement repulsed the woman he'd loved?

Jane glanced up, and their gazes locked. The connection was magnetic. As undeniable as it was untenable. Unacceptable. When she smiled, his stomach tensed, and all manner of emotional chaos pulled at his chest.

He instinctively smiled back.

Already in too deep, he made a deal with himself and the devil. Just through the holidays—maybe a little longer if Jane's family still hadn't been found—he'd stop overanalyzing every glance and touch. He'd stop obsessing over whether or not he was falling for her in favor of merely enjoying her company for whatever time they shared. What could that hurt? He'd view it as a sort of vacation—nothing more. Once she and the baby were gone, he'd resume his normal, gloomy existence.

No biggie, right?

He released a long, slow exhale.

Just keep telling yourself that, buddy. You're a fool to believe that if you repeat it enough, it might come true.

JANE FOUGHT a moment of panic when she left the nursery and didn't immediately find Gideon in the waiting area. But then she saw him, asleep in a corner chair. His long legs stretched in front of him. He'd tipped his black leather cowboy hat low to cover his eyes.

Her runaway pulse slowed.

He represented the only stability in her life.

Since Chip's nurse had been antsy to get him back under his medicinal light, Jane hadn't even been able to hold him as long as she would have liked.

Unsure whether to wake Gideon or find a magazine and sit beside him, letting him rest, she'd opted for the latter when the elevator dinged and a trio of teen girls giggled their way onto the floor.

Gideon woke with a start. "Oh, hey…"

His hat tumbled to the floor.

She picked it up, for a moment hugging it to her, enjoying his distinct smell of worn leather and the pine that laced the entire town.

When he rubbed his eyes, she couldn't help but grin at his hat head. He needed a haircut, but far be it from her to tell him.

"Hi. Sorry. I was going to let you sleep, but…" Her words trailed off when she hooked her thumb toward the three girls gaping at the babies through the nursery window.

"It's okay. Guess the past few days are catching up with me. How are you not more tired?"

"Adrenaline?" She sat beside him and handed over his hat. "I got booted out of the nursery. Should we head back to the inn for an official nap?"

"Sounds like a plan." He rose, slapped his hat squarely back on his head, then offered her his hand to help her to her feet. The gesture confused her on myriad levels. Was he just being polite? Or should she read something more into the way he held his fingers to hers a fraction of second longer than necessary? Her heart skipped a happy beat.

It took under fifteen minutes until they each stood in front of their respective rooms.

Jane found herself dreading the thought of being without him—even for an hour. Forcing a breath, she found the courage to say, "I, um, have a king-size bed.

Would you mind lying down with me for a little while? I don't want to be alone."

"Jane…" He stood ramrod straight with his hand on his door handle. "I'm not sure that's a good idea."

"Promise—I'm not putting moves on you. I just can't be alone. Last night, I barely slept at all, because every time I drifted off, I woke not knowing where or who I was." She bowed her head, searching for the right words to make him understand. "When I'm with you… I feel different. It's not about any sort of a man-woman attraction—" *although I'd be lying if I didn't admit to finding you awfully handsome* "—but deeper. A fundamental safety sort of thing."

A muscle ticked in his jaw. He stared hard at his door, as if it were the most fascinating door he'd ever encountered.

"Gideon, *please*…" Jane hated the whiny tone in her voice—the desperation. But she couldn't hide the terror welling inside her from the mere idea of waking up alone. "You can put pillows between us if you're afraid I might try something *unseemly*." She'd intended that last bit to be a joke, but honestly? Nothing would feel better than to drift off to sleep with him spooning her.

"Yeah, sure. What could it hurt, right? But if you do have a husband, I'd appreciate you keeping this just between us. Last thing I want is for some other guy having a beef with me for putting moves on his girl."

Relief shimmered through her. Before he changed his mind, she plunged her card key into her lock. "I'm not married."

"How do you know?"

I just know. "Can we please lie down? I'm exhausted."

"Me, too."

She kicked off her hiking boots—her only shoes—

then tugged back the comforter. Late-afternoon sun slanted through tall, paned windows. From outside came the faint sound of children laughing and carols still playing over the loudspeakers in Santa's park.

After fluffing two feather pillows, she climbed into the bed, tugging the sheet and quilt to her neck to ward off a sudden chill.

"This was a bad idea," Gideon said.

"Speak for yourself. This mattress is a cloud." She sighed with happiness.

He cleared his throat before approaching the bed.

"What are you waiting for?" she asked.

"Nothing." He rested beside her, only instead of sliding under the quilt, Gideon practically hung off the side. He even kept on his hat and boots, but was careful not to get his soles on the bed.

Jane said, "I don't have cooties."

"You might bite." She was sure he'd meant the quip as a joke, but the stern set of his mouth told another story. What was wrong?

"Maybe…" She, too, tried making light of the situation. How could she make him relax? "This is off topic, but after our nap, we'll still have time to kill before Chip's night feeding. I saw a sign for a spaghetti supper being held at a church down the street. Want to go? There's also going to be singing and a bell performance. I love those—the ethereal sound. I'm not sure how, but—"

"This isn't working." As if the quilt had caught fire, he bolted from the bed. "I have to go."

"What do you mean? Are you feeling okay?"

"Sorry. I just have to go."

Chapter Ten

Gideon didn't want a nap.

He wanted his leg back.

He wanted to not have to climb into bed beside a beautiful woman with his boots on. It was demoralizing.

He left Jane's room and strode down the hall, desperate for air. What did he desire even more than his leg? Not a damn thing that was platonic. He wanted to hold Jane, kiss her—do things in that big bed that no gentleman would ever ask of a woman who didn't even know her own name. It was shameful and wrong, and the knowing did nothing to stop the base wanting.

Outside, he breathed gallons of cool twilight air.

Above the town, the sky put on a brilliant show, streaked with purples, yellows and reds. Even as he ran from Jane, Gideon now craved sharing this beauty with her. They'd known each other only days. How had she already gotten under his skin?

He walked to the edge of town—not far, maybe two miles.

Along the way, he passed the historic white church hosting Jane's supper. Even from the street, conversation and laughter and music could be heard. The sweet smell of Italian sausage and garlic toast made his stomach growl.

A pang twisted his gut. A craving to once again be normal.

He and Missy used to go to way too much church with her grandmother. Back then, since he was so rarely home, he'd resented the time away from his jumbo TV, fishing boat and beer. The benefit of hindsight had no trouble telling him he'd been a fool. Still was a fool if he didn't get back to the inn and ask Jane to accompany him to a simple meal that was in his heart, extraordinarily complex.

JANE SAT CURLED up on the settee with the quilt and a bag of chips from the minibar when a knock sounded at the door.

"Go away!" she shouted as she turned the volume up on *Cake Wars*.

Ignoring her, he knocked again.

She sighed, then jerked open the door. "I don't want to see you,"

He stormed passed her, grabbed the remote and turned off the TV. "Tough."

"I'll call a cab to get to the hospital."

"Fine. But how are you going to pay for it?" Great question. Jane was so mad at him for leaving her, she hadn't fully thought her plan through.

"I'll figure it out."

He crossed the room and made the settee feel much too small when he sat beside her. He took off his hat, setting it in his lap, but running his fingers back and forth along the brim. "I'm sorry."

"Thank you." She fisted the quilt, hating that his hat hair was adorable. "Why did you go? It was just a nap."

"Because I respect you." He leaned his head back against the sofa. "I'll tell you the truth."

"I feel flattered."

"I don't blame you for being pissed. Hell…" He snorted. "I'm pissed. But here's the deal—I like you, Jane. And when we shared a bed, it—well, it didn't feel right."

"Nothing happened!" she said. "You're acting crazy. It was just a nap. Or, was going to be."

"I know. But what if I wanted it to be more?" He avoided her gaze.

"What are you talking about?" Her gaze widened. "Like…*hanky-panky*?"

He laughed. "I would have called it something else, but yeah. And that can't happen. Not only did you just have a baby, but you're married."

"Please stop with that. If I were married, where's my ring? And don't you think a husband might have noticed I'm gone?"

"Valid points. But I still don't think we should—"

Kiss? Hold hands? Someday, maybe more? She licked her lips. "Agreed. Which is why I asked you to take a nap. Nothing more."

"Good." He raked both hands through his hair and nodded. "We're on the same page."

"Absolutely." *But what if I don't like that page? What if I want a whole other book?*

"Now that we've got that out of the way, did you want to go to the spaghetti thing down at the church?"

"Sure. If it's not a date."

"Did I say it was? Because if you thought that, then—"

"Gideon, chill. I'm teasing. Relax." She reached toward him to pat his knee, but he flinched, then stood, planting his hat back on his head. "If we're going to eat before visiting the baby, we'd better go."

Because she was no longer sure what to say in the face of his downright bizarre behavior, Jane left the settee to find her boots.

"Hold up," he said. "This afternoon, while you were in the truck, I bought you a pair of running shoes. Figured they'd be more comfortable than lugging those around all the time."

He bought her shoes? What little remained of her anger faded. "How did you know my size?"

He'd ducked into his room and returned with a bulging sack. "When I did your laundry, I checked. Hope you don't mind, but I grabbed jeans. A few sweaters, too."

"Thank you." Blown away by his thoughtfulness, she pressed her hands over her swelling heart. "I'd hug you, but would that be allowed?"

"Sure. But don't get any ideas about grabbing my ass."

"You wish." She winked before hugging him for her gifts.

Fifteen minutes later, they were off. Her jeans and sweater were a little big, but her socks and sneakers fit like a dream.

The night was perfect for walking. Crisp temperatures laced with pine, but no wind. The wooden boardwalks teemed with families and couples either shopping or bustling to holiday events.

With Gideon by her side, Jane pretended she wasn't a guest in the town, but a full-time resident. A half dozen men stopped him with minor horse care questions. He answered them all with patience and ease, making her proud to be alongside him—even if they were only friends.

At the church, he paid the five-dollar admission fee

for them both, then donated an extra twenty. The food was served buffet-style out of the church's kitchen, which adjoined a wood-floored recreation area with a basketball hoop at one end and stage at the other. Dozens of round tables had been draped with white cloths. Mini Christmas trees sat at the center of each, along with heavy-handed red and green glitter. Elementary school–aged children darted in and out of the long food line, with parents alternately chatting with friends or scolding.

Bing Crosby crooned carols over a sound system, and hundreds of paper snowflakes twirled from the ceiling. A man dressed as Santa made the rounds, passing out candy canes with each stop.

If I never regain my memory, could this one day be my church? My man? She hoped so. She wanted his hand possessively pressed to the small of her back, guiding her through the line. She wanted them to know everyone in the entire congregation and feel part of an institution so much larger than themselves.

"Well, I'll be damned. If it isn't this town's biggest heathen." A towering man dressed in a beige law enforcement uniform, wearing a sheriff's badge, pumped Gideon's hand. "And you must be our famous Jane Doe?"

"Ignore him," Gideon urged. "He might be the sheriff now, but he's up for reelection and sure as hell won't get my vote."

Jane had known Gideon long enough to recognize when he was teasing. It was her guess that the men were close friends.

"I should have known all the profanity was coming from this part of the line." A blonde stepped up, landing playful swats on both of the guys' shoulders.

She looked to be about six months pregnant. Her pink maternity dress strained at her belly. Her smile was as radiant as her shining blue eyes when she held out her hand to Jane. "Hi. I'm Sherrie. Please accept my apology in advance for anything crude, oafish or disgusting that may leave West's mouth. My husband may be great at his job, but polite conversation has never been his strongest asset."

West quipped, "See if I vote for you come November."

Sherrie rolled her eyes.

"Nice to meet you," Jane said, glad for female companionship. "What office are you running for?"

"Mayor," West said with a chest swelled with pride. "At least until I vote for her opposition."

"What neither of them is telling you," Gideon interjected, "is that they've both run unopposed for their last three terms. Everyone loves them."

"Stop." Sherrie took a tray and plate from a stack at the end of the line. "I'm blessed to have the trust of my friends and neighbors."

"Likewise," West said. "But dinner conversations get heated if we don't see eye to eye on certain issues—like speed bumps."

"Here we go…" Gideon took two trays and plates, handing a set to Jane. "Never, ever get them started on those damned speed bumps. It's been the most hotly debated political issue in town since the old mayor got booted from office over his wife changing the traditional Fourth of July bunting from red, white and blue to just white."

They moved up in line to the silverware and napkins.

Sherrie made the sign of the cross on her chest, glancing heavenward. "That year, we had biblical rains over the three-day holiday weekend. The sun came out just in time for the annual parade, but the décor was muddy gray. I won my election in a landslide by promising to bring back the old bunting."

"It didn't hurt her cause," West said, "that Mayor Franks was ninety-two and also planned to close off all of downtown to motorized traffic."

"I still don't think that's a bad idea," Sherrie said. "Could be just the thing to boost tourism."

"I'm begging you, don't try it," West teased. Patting her baby bump, he added, "Unless you want to be a stay-at-home mom?"

Sherrie stuck out her tongue at her husband.

He kissed her.

A pang tore through Jane over the couple's playful banter. She wanted a relationship like that. One in which there was plenty of laughter, but she wasn't afraid to speak her mind on any given subject.

There was no more time for talk while they made their food selections. Three perfectly plump grandmotherly types in frilly aprons served Caesar salad, pasta topped with a thick red sauce, and a choice of meatballs, Italian sausage or grilled chicken for toppings. There was garlic toast and fresh-grated Parmesan, plus tiramisu or cheesecake for dessert.

With his sweet tooth, Gideon chose both.

Sherrie landed at the nearest open table and was joined by her husband. Gideon followed, setting his tray on their table before taking Jane's tray from her, then pulling out her chair.

"Look how sweet Gideon is," Sherrie said, nudging her hubby with her shoulder. "Unlike West, he actually remembers the manners his mother taught him."

West ignored her jab in favor of digging into his platter of spaghetti with all three meats.

"Gideon, you've never told us much about your family," Sherrie said. "Where are they?"

"In their graves."

The mayor paled, dropping her fork clanging to her plate. "I'm so sorry. West never told me." She elbowed her husband, adding a dirty look for good measure.

"It is what it is." Gideon started his meal with cheesecake.

Jane's heart ached for him.

Under the table, she put her hand on his right thigh. To her shock—and delight—he covered her hand with his, giving her a light squeeze. More than the company or food, she appreciated this secret connection. She loved that he knew she was there for him. That she remembered their intimate campfire conversation about his mother and how she'd constantly let him down. He could have bad-mouthed her, but didn't. In his strong, stoic way, he shouldered the pain. Or maybe he masked it by eating his dessert first. Either way, she found herself admiring him more.

They were finishing their meals when the stage curtain opened, revealing a red-robed children's choir. Their rendition of "Ave Maria" gave Jane happy chills. Had there ever been a more perfect night? The only thing that would make it better would be holding Chip in her arms.

When the bell players performed, their notes were crystalline and pure.

Jane couldn't have said why, but beneath the table she clasped Gideon's hand and once again, he didn't fight her. In that moment, she needed the human connection. She needed to know she wasn't alone in her appreciation of her current blessings.

At this moment, she didn't want her memory to return. All she truly wanted was for this magical night with Gideon and her new friends to never end.

Sadly, it soon enough did.

The temperature had dipped into the lower twenties, so while West drove off to sort out a bar brawl, Sherrie offered to give Gideon and Jane a ride to the inn.

From there, the two hopped in his truck for the short trip to the hospital to feed her son.

The other two infants had gone home, meaning the nursery was empty save for Chip and two nurses who sat at a desk at the far end of the L-shaped room.

With Gideon in the waiting area, Jane sat in a rocker, nursing her son, telling him about her night. "You should have seen how serious all the kids looked in their robes," she whispered in a playful tone. "Except for the one boy on the end who looked like he'd forgotten to brush his hair. Of course, I didn't say anything to Gideon, but a part of me wondered if that might have been him as a little boy. You know, with his mom not helping him prepare for concerts. Even worse, maybe he didn't have any performances at all?" Chip's eyes widened, keeping a firm grip on Jane's pinkie. "How sad would that have been?"

Of course, her son didn't answer, but the question hurt Jane all the same. What would it take for her to vanquish the haunted expression she sometimes caught in Gideon's gaze?

Was it any of her business?

The question caught her off guard.

Technically, no. She had no say in anything he felt or did. But he had saved her and her son's lives. That had to count for something. That forged a unique bond between them that even he couldn't ignore.

What that said about their future? Too soon to tell. But one thing was growing painfully clear—when it came to Gideon, she very much wanted him to share her future.

As for her past? It was too terrifying to face, so she'd rather ignore it. Besides, in life, there was no such thing as going backward—only forward. Forward into a bright and shiny new life with Gideon Snow.

BACK AT THE INN, outside their rooms, Gideon wasn't sure what to do with his hands. It had been a long night, but he found himself not wanting it to end. Should he see if maybe Jane wanted to join him in catching a movie? The inn offered HBO. Cable was a luxury they wouldn't have once they got to the cabin.

"Well…" She covered her mouth through a yawn. "I guess we should get some rest."

"Are you—"

"I want to—"

They laughed after speaking over each other.

"You first," Gideon said.

"I wanted to thank you for a fun night. The food, the company, the children's performances—all of it was perfect."

"You're welcome. Glad you enjoyed it." *Ask her to your room for a movie, idiot. She just said she had a good time. Why not keep it going?* "Sorry about Sherrie and West. They're a handful."

"Are you kidding? They're a great couple. I would give anything to share that kind of closeness with someone someday."

I used to have it. Till my pride and Missy's hollow heart threw it away.

"Do you ever want to remarry?"

"No." Even if his leg—or lack thereof—weren't an issue, his screwed-up head was. Aside from horses, he was no use to anyone.

"That makes me sad."

"Why do you care?" Bitterness seeped into his tone. The pretty smile she'd worn all night faded. It killed him that he'd done that to her. It killed him that he would never be the sort of stand-up guy like West who knew how to keep a woman happy.

Jane sighed. "I'm tired. See you in the morning."

She fit her key into the reader, entered her room and closed the door behind her.

He was still standing there when he heard the jangle of her chain lock.

Idiot.

So much for his movie. But then watching a movie with Jane had never really been the issue. The true problem was that this went deeper than one night. He liked eating with her and shopping with her and laughing and talking and spending time as a couple with his best friends. Only what would it take for his thick skull to realize he and Jane weren't a couple now, and they never would be?

Chapter Eleven

"Here it is…" Gideon opened his cabin's front door and stepped back, holding out his arm for Jane to enter. "Home sweet home—at least until your family shows up to save you."

"This is cute," she said. "Why would I need saving?" It was late afternoon before Chip had been discharged from the hospital. They both had an appointment the next week to see Dr. Childress—a general practitioner assigned to her case. Gideon had met him a few times around town. He seemed like an all right guy, or he would have suggested Jane see someone else.

Darkness had fallen. There were no lights on, and it was cold enough to see his breath in the moonlight. He should have called ahead to have Mrs. Gentry start a fire or make a meal. This was one time when he wouldn't have minded her nosing around.

"You haven't seen it yet. It's dark."

"The outside is adorable. And it smells good. Like woodsmoke and you."

"I have a smell?" He brushed past her, closing the door before turning on the kitchen's overhead light.

"Everyone does. Oh—this is darling. Are the cabinets original?"

"Yes. Well, except for the granite. I gutted the original bathroom, and my contractor talked me into adding new kitchen counters. Said it would be best for resale."

"Are you planning on selling?"

"Not soon. Maybe never. But it doesn't hurt to keep my options open."

"True..." She skimmed her fingers almost reverently over the nearest cabinet's glossy finish. Half of the doors were solid. The other half had eight-paned glass fronts. "Imagine the history these have seen."

He had to laugh. "This place used to be a stopover for bootleggers. The history might not have been kid-friendly."

Chip was surprisingly alert, peering at his new surroundings and Gideon.

"I doubt he'll be scarred too badly." With one last look at the kitchen, Jane said, "Let me help you carry in Chip's swing. We'll let him play a bit while we haul the rest of his things."

"I can get all of it. You stay inside where it's warm."

"Hate to break it to you," she said, "but I think it's colder in here than it is outside. Maybe our first order of business should be building a fire."

"Or I could just turn up the heat." He aimed for the thermostat that hung on the wall between the bedroom and bathroom. "No wonder it's cold. It's set on sixty."

"Funny how that seems like a perfect temp when you're out in the sun, but inside, it's chilly."

"Hungry?"

"Not especially." They stood on opposite sides of the kitchen counter that served as a room divider between the kitchen and living room. Having her on his home turf felt beyond uncomfortable. He wasn't sure what to do or say. Where to put his hands. "I'll start unloading."

"I'll help."

"I'd prefer you stay inside with the baby. Let's get you two set up in the bedroom. I'll sleep on the sofa."

"That's not fair."

"Isn't about what's fair, but sheer necessity. There's no telling how many times the little bugger will need you in the night. Besides, he has a lot of gear. You'll need the space."

"Why don't we share the bed? You know how I feel about being alone."

"Out of the question." He turned his back to her. "I'll be in the barn. Unload or don't. I don't care."

JANE STARED AT the closed door and took a page from her new friend Sherrie's book by sticking her tongue out at her man. Didn't matter that Gideon wasn't hers and would never be. For the moment, they were stuck together. Couldn't he at least be civil?

What was wrong about sharing a bed? And if more *sharing* happened, would that be so bad?

Chip cooed, wriggling in her arms.

"Ready for a stretch, angel?" Spying an afghan on the back of the couch, she spread it on the oval braided rug covering most of the living room's hardwood floor. Lying the baby on top, she unwrapped his blanket, then rested him on his tummy. "Stay here, sweetie. I'll be right back."

It took three trips to gather Chip's gear from the truck's bed. Three more trips to haul it all into the bedroom. By then, the heat had kicked on and the cabin felt more like the tropics than a mountain hideaway.

Jane was so angry with Gideon's latest tantrum that she had no qualms about taking the bedroom for herself. Screw him.

Putting her energy into assembling the bassinet's

legs, with the aid of a screwdriver she found in a kitchen junk drawer, Jane finished the task in under ten minutes.

Back in the living room, she asked Chip, "What did I ever find attractive about him?"

She scooped her son from his blanket and collapsed onto the comfy leather sofa, cradling him in her arms. "I mean, he's got this whole Dr. Jekyll/Mr. Hyde thing going that's starting to be a real drag. One minute, he's sweetest man alive, the next…" She growled. "I'm so mad I can't even think of an appropriately bad word to describe him."

"Want me to give you a few?" He emerged from the bathroom.

"You scared me." She clutched her chest. "When did you come inside?"

"Long enough to know that instead of sleeping on the couch, I'll be in the doghouse—at least, I would if I had one. Would the chicken coop be low enough?"

"Ha! I wouldn't punish the poor chickens by making them put up with you."

"That hurts." He feigned a pained expression. "But as usual, I've got it coming. You just have this knack for—"

"Wait—you're apologizing by telling me I'm the one with a problem?"

"Forget I said anything. I'm starving. Want me to make us a couple sandwiches?"

"Let me. You work on a fire. Now that I've sat down, it's still chilly."

"Yes, ma'am."

She placed a yawning Chip in his comfy new carrier, then found deli shaved ham and Swiss cheese in the fridge. "Are you a mustard or mayo guy?"

"Both, please. And bread-and-butter pickles—lots."

Way in the back on the top shelf, she found a half-full jar. "Who made these for you?"

"My crazy neighbor. Mrs. Gentry—remember? I told you about her. I'm sure you'll meet her in the morning. Most days, she's a godsend. Seems to actually enjoy keeping my fridge stocked and helping with my livestock when I'm not around. I've tried paying her, but she insists all she wants are half of my eggs—which she then uses by cooking for me."

"She sounds amazing. You're lucky to have her—especially if you're as crotchety with her as you are me."

"True." He stopped adding logs to the fire to sit on the stone hearth. "I don't mean to be. I'm working on it—being more even-keeled. But it's hard. I've lived alone for so long that sometimes I forget that being around others is a give-and-take."

"What was she like?" Jane dared ask.

"Who? My wife?"

Throat tight, she nodded before slicing a tomato.

His lips curved into a sentimental grin she hadn't before seen. "She was a ballbuster. Actually, a lot like you. Never let me get away with shit."

"I like her."

"She would have liked you." He placed smaller sticks and rolled paper under the logs.

"If she were still alive, would you try getting her back?"

"Damn, you go for the jugular."

"Sorry." She spread condiments on thick slabs of homemade wheat bread. Another gift from Mrs. Gentry?

"Hell, I don't know." He took matches from a box, lit one, then held it to the paper. It lit, and soon flames danced and crackled. "Maybe. Probably. There are a lot of factors you wouldn't understand—I still don't."

"Fair enough." She opened and closed cabinets until finding two plates. She placed the sandwiches on them, then looked through a pantry for chips, adding a handful to each plate before taking both in hand. She passed Gideon his. "Sorry I pried. I was curious."

"Thanks." He'd already taken a bite of his sandwich. "It was a legit question. Wish I'd had the chance to know."

"Since you didn't—" she put down her sandwich to lift Chip out of his carrier and onto the sofa beside her "—have you ever considered giving yourself a break?"

"What do you mean?"

"I mean a do-over—like what this whole lost memory thing has done for me. Think about it—logically, there can't have been a happy reason for me hiking that far out, that close to my due date, but I did. By a miracle or twist of fate or whatever you want to call it, you charged in to my rescue and saved my life. And now I have a clean slate. No messy baggage. No regrets over exes—at least, none that I know of. And so here I sit, a textbook case of second chances." She ate a potato chip. "Heck, if you want, feel free to join me."

"How am I supposed to do that?" In the time it had taken to make her speech, he'd finished his meal.

"Make a conscious decision to do it—start over. From this very moment, forgive yourself for whatever part you played in your divorce and start fresh."

"It's not that easy."

"Yes, Gideon, it is."

He stood, taking his plate to the sink. "What you're forgetting is that I didn't conveniently conk my head on a rock. But I tell you what, I like your idea enough to give it a try."

"Really?" She raised her eyebrows. "You're not just saying that to get me off your back?"

"You think that little of me?" He popped into the narrow pantry cabinet, emerging with two bags of cookies. After wagging the bags, he asked, "Oatmeal or chocolate chip?"

"We were having a serious conversation."

"My question is serious."

"Never mind. I'm going to feed the baby and then go to bed."

"It's seven o'clock." He crammed a chocolate chip cookie into his mouth.

"Who appointed you the bedroom police?"

"I don't have an official title," he said with a slow grin and tip of his cowboy hat that made it impossible for her to stay mad. "But with any luck, that day will come."

"You're horrible."

He'd returned to the living room, sitting uncomfortably close, again offering her choice of bags. "How can any man offering cookies be all bad?"

"You just are." She chose oatmeal.

"But you still love me." His right side touched her left. Scalded her. Made her far too aware of the fact that he was a man and she was a woman.

She knew he'd meant the words as a joke. So did he.

But neither was smiling, and her heart beat way too fast. How different everything would be if he did love her. They'd stop this petty bickering and go to bed together, where they'd do anything but sleep.

Just thinking about the myriad ways she'd like to touch him superheated her cheeks.

"You all right?" he asked, leaning close enough that a slip of paper couldn't have passed between them.

"Fine. Give me another cookie."

"Why would I do that? You didn't say please..." She turned to snap a sassy reply, but he was right there. The only thing keeping their lips from accidentally colliding was his cowboy hat's brim. His breath smelled of chocolate chips. His dark gaze proved as temptingly sweet. Her lips tingled, her pulse pounded, and her lungs forgot how to breathe. "Haven't you heard it's impolite to wear your hat in the house?"

"Where did you get the impression I'm polite?"

"You're impossible." Her voice sounded more like a squeak. Like she was a tiny mouse and he was a hungry cougar. No, he wasn't polite. He was maddeningly complex. At times, a lovable lug. Other times infuriating to the point that he needed a good slap. Regardless, she fought the urge to take off his hat, fling it across the room, then have her way with him. The doctor may have said it would be six weeks before she could resume normal bedroom activity, but between her and Gideon, what constituted normal?

Hands on her knees, fingers digging in to force herself not to touch Gideon, she turned away from him to look at her son. Her baby represented safety—*sanity.*

"Seems strange..." He finished another cookie.

"What?"

"How it's only a little over three weeks till Christmas—the whole town is on holiday steroids. Yet there's no sign of it in here. Want me to cut us a tree in the morning?"

"Y-yes, please." Just like that, he was back in her good graces—not that he'd ever fully been out.

What was she going to do with herself? How long

would she reside in this purgatory of not knowing her name or true heart? For no logical reason, she was falling for Gideon, but to what end? "I-I need to ask you a question."

"Shoot."

"If…" Her mouth dried. Her tongue forgot to speak. "If we hadn't met under such unconventional circumstances. Say Sherrie and West had introduced us on a blind date. Would you be interested in me as a woman, or friend?" She faced him straight on, needing to not just hear his answer, but to see his reaction to it play out on his face.

"God's honest truth?"

"Yes. Please."

"Damn…" Now he was the one looking away. Was he scared? Of what? "It's like this: I'm not in the market for anything more than friendship—never will be. But if I did want to be…"

"You make me crazy. Why can't you answer the question?"

"Why can't you let things be? Lord, woman. Why does everything have to be analyzed to death? Why can't we just sit here on the sofa and share cookies? Why are you so damned complicated?"

"Me?" She laughed. "I'm an open book, clean slate, pure as the driven snow. You, on the other hand—"

"Did I ever claim to be a saint? Haven't I told you from the start I'm fu—messed up?" He'd raised his voice—not a lot, but enough to alert her to the fact that this had grown heated.

Hands to her temples, Jane squeezed her eyes to sudden, screaming pain.

It's done. Cry all you want. It won't make a difference.

"Jane?" Gideon flung off his hat, cupping her face

between his hands. "Can you hear me? Are you okay? Do you need an ambulance?"

As fast as the pain had come, it was now gone, along with the masculine voice that had been raging in her head.

Silent tears streamed down her cheeks. She didn't know why she was crying, only that her soul felt consumed by the feeling that something important had been ripped from her. But what?

"Jane? Baby, talk to me." He slid his hands to her shoulders, giving her a barely perceptible shake. "Jane?"

"I'm—I'm good." Sort of.

"What happened?"

"I don't know. You and I were arguing, but then there was a burst in my head, and I heard you, but also another man's voice. He told me it was *done*. That it didn't matter how much I cried. It was over. Could he have been talking about our marriage? Was I married? Was that why I ran away? Because he didn't want me or our child?"

Gideon didn't just hug her, but placed the sleeping baby into his carrier before pulling her onto his lap. Rocking her, whispering into the fall of her hair that everything would be okay. Because she looked to him for all things good in her life, Jane blindly believed him.

And if she had been married? If her memory flash was to be believed, that marriage was over now, making her free to pursue this life with Gideon. He said he had no interest in a romantic relationship, but what if she changed his mind?

Chapter Twelve

The next morning, Gideon tugged open the barn door, leading Jane and the baby inside. He wasn't going to lie; despite her delicious French toast breakfast, her headache and the sliver of her memory returning had him on edge. He'd slept about five minutes and felt like shit, but that didn't give him a pass on caring for his livestock.

"This is the infamous Jelly Bean." He forced an upbeat tone.

"You caused us a lot of trouble." Jane stroked the horse's nose. "But it's okay. I'm sure you were scared by the storm."

"No excuses," he said. "The whole reason she's here is to get her not to spook." He saw a parallel between the mare and Jane. They'd both been through trauma. He had no doubt he could one day make the horse whole, but with Jane he may be in over his head.

"Don't listen to Mr. Cranky Pants," Jane cooed. She looked pretty in her new jeans and red sweater. A couple years earlier, Mrs. Gentry had crocheted him a red-and-white-striped beanie cap. It looked way cuter on Jane than it had him. She also wore the matching mittens.

Chip was decked out in an adorable red snowsuit that made him look like a mini Santa.

"If you'd feed the chickens and donkey, I'll work with Jelly Bean."

"Um, I'm happy to help, but will need guidance. What does everyone eat and how much? Where is the food—those kinds of things."

He got Jane lined up, filled a feed trough with hay to set the baby in, then worked with Jelly Bean. The horse was skittish in the paddock. The storm had set them back in terms of trust. She seemed fine in her stall, but didn't like the open space.

Once Jane had fed the donkey, Gideon led the docile creature into the paddock. The plan was to show Jelly Bean she had nothing to fear by example. This was a waiting game. Gideon stood in the paddock's center, softly chattering about nonsense, because that was what the horse had enjoyed when Angela had been alive. While Jelly Bean snorted and charged, Fred the donkey contentedly munched a handful of hay.

"Chickens are— Shouldn't you get out of there?" Jane had rounded the corner from the barn and held the baby in her arms. She stood at the fence, wide-eyed with concern. "That looks dangerous."

"I'm fine. Trying to teach her that I'm safe. Being outside is safe. Ironically, when she first got here she was afraid of the barn. Now it's the other way around. Once she calms, I have a few more exercises to lead her through, then we'll look for the Christmas tree."

"I'm not in a hurry," Jane said.

I am. With her watching, he felt as nervous as the horse. He'd worked a year in physical therapy to walk without a limp, but every so often it happened. Would she notice? Would she care? Why did he care what she thought? Why couldn't he shake the feeling that without her and the baby, his life might never be the same?

And that was a bad thing. Her memory flash was no doubt the first of many. Would they come faster and faster until her entire past rushed forward? Did they have days together or weeks?

"It's cold," he said. "Shouldn't you take Chip inside?"

"He's fine. One of my favorite nurses told me a good rule of thumb is that babies feel the same temperature as we do. As long as we're comfy, he should be, too."

That wasn't what Gideon wanted to hear.

He wanted Jane and the baby back in the cabin so he wouldn't fantasize about what it might be like to teach Chip to ride. But what were the odds of Jane's memory holding off that long? She hadn't lived in a vacuum. Somewhere, someone had to be missing her. If it wasn't her former husband, then a boss or neighbor? Her parents or siblings? Even her obstetrician was a possible connection. Wouldn't a doctor find it odd that a patient so close to delivery vanished?

An engine revved, spooking the horse. Gideon muttered a string of curses under his breath.

Mrs. Gentry approached on her red four-wheeler. Spotting him, she waved.

Great. Just what he needed.

She killed the engine and jumped off, zeroing in on the baby. "You must be Jane and itty-bitty Chip. I've been so excited to meet both of you." She wiggled the baby's foot.

"Hi," Jane said. "You must be the famous Mrs. Gentry. I enjoyed your homemade bread for breakfast and dinner, and I'm loving your hat."

Mrs. Gentry beamed. "Thank you. I can tell we'll be great friends. Gideon is about as welcoming as a tough old goat, but stick with me and you'll feel right at home."

"Thank you."

While the women chatted and fussed over the baby, the sun rose higher, the air warmed, and the sky opened into a radiant blue. The whole world sounded as if it were dripping with melting snow.

Gideon sensed the mare had had enough for the day, so he walked her into the barn, brushed her, gave her a drink and a few handfuls of grain.

"I hear we're going for a Christmas tree," Mrs. Gentry said when he rejoined them. "Jane, do you think a six-footer would fit in that alcove by the front window?"

She wrinkled her nose. "I'm horrible with those kinds of measurements."

"How do you know?"

"Good question," Jane said with a laugh. After last night's episode, he would have expected her to be on edge, fearing another. To the contrary, she'd made a delicious French toast breakfast, fed, bathed, and clothed the baby, and was then game to help with chores.

"Just to be sure," Mrs. Gentry said, "let's measure. Gideon keeps a tape in the utility closet toolbox."

Gideon joined the women on the walk to the cabin. Midway, he asked his nosy neighbor, "Have you thought about getting help for your boundary issues?"

"What do you mean?" When Mrs. Gentry looked confused by his question, Gideon laughed it off.

He was secretly glad to see Jane hiding a smile.

After much debate, it was decided that their tree should be a seven-footer. Since there was still at least eight inches of snow on the ground, the four of them struck out on the mostly clear trail leading from his cabin to federal land. With at least a square mile before they reached the park, they had plenty of trees to choose from.

"How about that one?" Gideon asked after a ten-minute hike.

"It's got a bald spot," Mrs. Gentry complained.

"That one?" Gideon asked five minutes later.

"Too short." Jane had passed the baby to Mrs. Gentry while she used the tape measure to get an official reading.

Fifteen minutes after that, he pointed to a good-looking fir with which neither of the women could possibly find fault.

"Too stubby," Jane said.

"I concur." Mrs. Gentry waved her free arm. "This is Baby Chip's first Christmas. His tree should feel grand."

Gideon growled.

Thirty minutes' worth of hiking in circles, uphill, downhill, around boulders and through a ravine, Jane finally stopped in front of a noble fir that to Gideon looked identical to the last forty she'd inspected.

"That's the one," she announced. "Mrs. Gentry? Do you agree?"

"Absolutely." She showed her support by clapping Chip's mitten-covered hands. "It's divine."

Divine? Since when had his four-wheel driving, boot-wearing neighbor turned girlie girl?

Gideon asked, "You two are both sure?"

They nodded.

He cut.

An hour later and two wrong turns finally led them back to the cabin.

While Chip chilled in his swing and Gideon trimmed the tree and made a stand from a cut milk jug and scrap lumber he'd found in the barn, Mrs. Gentry taught Jane to make cocoa from scratch.

After Gideon hauled in the tree and placed it where the women decreed, he was more than happy to finally have a seat and relax, breathing in the tree's admittedly wonderful aroma.

"What about lights?" Mrs. Gentry asked.

Gideon groaned.

"I'll do them," Jane volunteered. "You rest." She handed him a steaming mug filled with chocolaty-smelling goodness. His first sip lifted him to sugar heaven. By his second and third sips, guilt assailed him for not helping Jane dig through the bags of baby paraphernalia, clothes, and lastly, Christmas lights.

"Why didn't you put all of that up last night?" Mrs. Gentry asked with a disapproving glare. "A baby needs structure."

"We were tired," Jane said. "We'd planned to do it this morning, but then—"

"You don't owe her an explanation," Gideon said. "In fact, Mrs. Gentry, isn't it about time for you to go?"

"But the tree isn't decorated yet."

"It'll be a while. We'll call when it's done. Besides, Chip needs lunch."

"I'll be happy to feed him," she said.

"I'm breastfeeding," Jane reminded.

"Oh—I forgot." Her eyebrows raised to her hairline. "Wait—are you two an item? Do you want to be alone?" She snatched her purse from the kitchen counter, sprinting for the door. "Jane, call me. We need to plan for Christmas dinner. I like your idea to invite Sherrie and West and as many more friends as we can find. It will be fun."

"Whoa—Mrs. Gentry, you've got this all wrong." Gideon hopped to his feet for damage control. In the process, he spilled cocoa on his favorite red plaid shirt.

"Jane and I—we're not, well, much of anything. And when was someone going to tell me about this dinner plan?"

Mrs. Gentry kissed his cheek. "Sorry, angel. But we decided this was strictly need-to-know type intel. Hate to break it to you, but you don't need to know."

"The hell I don't. Especially if you plan on packing my cabin with all those folks."

"Actually…" Jane grinned. "We were thinking it might be extra festive to have a big potluck dinner in the barn. Set up tables on sawhorses and have everyone bring something. Doesn't that sound amazing?"

No. What was amazing? The size of her smile. The way her green eyes crinkled at the corners and her complexion glowed. In that moment, he would do anything to keep her smiling—the least of which was spending an afternoon with friends out in his drafty old barn.

"Gideon?" she asked. "You're okay with it, right?"

He nodded. "If that's what you want, we'll do it. Tell me how much money you need or what setup chores you need me to do."

"I'll do all the shopping and give you the receipts." Mrs. Gentry waved before rocketing out the door. "Bye!"

Jane covered her face with her hands. "I'm sorry if this is too much. While you were working with Jelly Bean, Mrs. Gentry asked about our plans for Christmas, and when I said we didn't have any, she tossed out a few ideas and I guess we got carried away."

"It's all right," he said. "Really. Hell, maybe it will be fun?"

"You think?"

"Nope. But for you, I promise to try."

"Thank you." She ambushed him with a hug. "We'll have an awesome day."

He growled.

IT WAS DARK when Jane finished putting lights on the tree. Gideon offered to help, but every time he stood behind her on the ladder, she'd suffered hot flashes and an urge to turn and kiss him that was too overwhelming for it to be safe.

Instead, he'd made a crackling fire. Put slow country carols on his satellite radio, and played peekaboo with Chip until her heart neared bursting with fullness.

"Know what we need?" he asked.

"What?" Hands on her hips, she stood back to admire her handiwork. If she said so herself, the tree looked beautiful—even without ornaments.

"This…" Holding the baby in the crook of one arm, he fished a small wrapped box from behind a sofa cushion, then stood to hand it to her. "Merry early Christmas."

"Gideon…" Her heart skipped a few beats. "What did you do?"

"It's not all that great. Just a little something to help you remember Chip's first holiday."

Hands trembling, she took her time tearing into the gold foil paper. "W-when did you get this?"

"Last night, while you were feeding the little man. The hospital gift shop was still open. I saw this and thought… Doesn't matter what I thought. Open it." He waved her along.

"Right. Sorry." She finished with the paper and opened the box. Nestled on a bed of white velvet was a crystal snowflake. The center had been engraved with the words Baby's 1st Christmas.

Tears welled in Jane's eyes. "Gideon...this is beyond sweet. Thank you."

"You're welcome. It's no big deal."

"Yes, it is. I love it. And when he's seventeen and has his girlfriend over, helping us decorate our tree, I can use it as a prompt for launching into his most embarrassing baby and toddler stories."

"Did you hear that, little man?" He held out the baby to consult him. "Your mommy is actively plotting against your love life. But don't you worry. Uncle Gideon will always have your back."

Uncle? Daddy would have a better ring.

All in good time. After he experienced what would be the quintessentially perfect holidays, he'd never want to let either of them go. Screw her past. She chose the present.

"Help me hang it on the tree," Jane said.

Gideon stood, settling the baby on his hip.

"Where do you think it should go?"

"There." She pointed to a spot about a foot from the top, facing the fire so the crystal caught the glow.

"You heard your mom, little man." Gideon made a show out of pretending the baby hung the satin loop on her appointed branch. "You should get used to following her commands."

"Stop." She swatted his arm, but upon touching his biceps, the playful gesture seemed more like she was copping a feel. Was he that rock hard all over? What she wouldn't give to know.

"Now what?" Gideon asked once the ornament was hung.

"We string popcorn."

"What if I don't have any?"

"We move on to plan B."

"Which is?" He shifted close enough that she wasn't sure if their arms touched or their auras. Regardless, a reckless longing stirred in her heart to press herself against him.

"Stringing cranberries."

"Fresh out of those, too." Had she imagined him leaning his head closer? As if he might want to kiss her as much as she wanted him to?

"What do you have?" Her words fell in a breathless tumble.

A crush on you...

What she wouldn't give to hear the phrase leave his perfectly kissable lips.

"You mean in regard to decorating the tree? Not much. But after chores, I'll take you to the store in the morning. Buy whatever you want. Missy loved the holidays. She had me stringing garland and lights over every square inch of our house."

Jane's hope sank like a rowboat with a slow leak. Except Gideon was her boat. Her only security. Who had a nasty habit of bringing his dead ex-wife into far too many conversations. Was that why he didn't seem interested in starting anything with her?

Because his heart was six feet under in a casket?

Chapter Thirteen

"Woman, you are spoiling me." Gideon pushed back his plate with a contented sigh. With the last of Mrs. Gentry's bread, Jane made French toast again. She'd added cinnamon and nutmeg and powdered sugar he hadn't even known he had. Maybe having Mrs. Gentry always hanging around and bringing him stuff wasn't such a bad thing?

"That's my goal. I want you so happy Chip and I are here that you never let us go."

"Jane..." He groaned before finishing the coffee she'd brewed—also delicious.

"I know, I know, you're convinced that any minute now, some man is going to charge in here and steal me away. But after that snippet of memory I had?" She shivered from her seat across the table. "Even if an ex did show up, why would I want to go with him?"

"But this isn't your home." Softening his voice, he said, "Don't get me wrong, as much as it pains me to admit, I could get used to having you and the little man around. And up until Christmas, I vote for more good eating and fun. But after? West knows people with the forestry service. They're going to start a search for the car you used to get you to your trail."

"Do you ever shut up?" She'd been using his iPad to

scroll through homemade ornament tips and Christmas cookie recipes, and now smacked the table hard enough for the tablet to jump.

Gideon dropped his fork to his plate and held up his hands. "Don't kill the messenger. I'm not trying to get rid of you. Just stating facts."

"You think I don't know them?"

"We're playing an elaborate game of house." Only this thing they'd created—whatever it was—wasn't even built of cards. More like tissue paper. "I'll be the first to admit, we're getting good at it. I loved putting Chip's ornament on the tree with you and sharing breakfast with you, but sooner or later, you and I should discuss a game plan for finding your true home. If we both put time into it, it can't be that hard."

"Not today." She pressed the heels of her hands to her forehead.

Elbows on the table, he leaned in. "Are you having another flashback?"

"No. Just a plain old tension headache—brought on by you. I thought we were having a pleasant morning. I'm almost done with our shopping list. Why do you have to be such a happy smasher?"

"Babe…" The endearment slipped out. Gideon wasn't sure where it had come from, but there it was. Hanging between them like an egg poised to drop and splatter.

A smile opened like petals on Jane's face. Eyebrows raised, she said, *"Babe?"*

"Slip of the tongue. No big deal."

"Okay…" She may have returned to her recipe hunt, but he didn't believe for one second that she wasn't filing his snafu for future ammunition.

THAT AFTERNOON, GIDEON loaded the last grocery bag from Kingman's into the truck bed and looked up. When he'd worked with Jelly Bean that morning, the sky had been blue. Sometime between then and now, angry gray blocked the sun, but it hadn't dampened Jane's mood.

She and Chip had sung to the chickens. The baby supervised from his hay-filled trough while she'd mucked stalls and brushed the donkey.

Jelly Bean was still skittish, but better. Gideon would try saddling her again in the next few days. Until then, he'd put himself at Jane's disposal. Whatever she needed, he'd give. Fingers crossed, there would be no more memory flashes. He'd survive without her, but life around his place was sure a lot brighter with her and her son.

When he'd slipped and called her babe, he'd been mortified. He'd used the same endearment as he had with his ex. In the moment, it had felt natural. Right. Just as it once had with Missy. What did that say about him? The women had a few similarities, but were otherwise nothing alike. In no way interchangeable. But the base feelings of comfortableness were the same. Maybe he'd only been responding to those?

He pushed the cart back up to the corral at the store's front, then climbed in the truck beside Jane. Per Chip's safety seat instructions, Gideon had turned off his truck's passenger-side airbag, then strapped him in. Meaning each time Jane sat in the middle, their shoulders jostled with every bump and pothole. Their thighs pressed when leaning into turns.

"That was exhausting," Jane said when he climbed in beside her. "I'm not complaining, but I didn't expect it to take that long."

"It was all those recipes you found."

"Cookie recipes—for you."

"I can't wait to taste-test every one."

Jane switched on the heat, and soon the air in the cab was balmy compared to the outside chill.

"So… I was thinking about Christmas dinner."

"What about it?" He finally maneuvered out of Kingman's hectic lot and onto the main road.

"Is there anyone else you'd like to invite?"

"Nope. Besides, seems like we've got a big enough gaggle of folks coming as is."

"True. I just thought you might have extended family you haven't connected with in a while? Old Navy buddies?"

"I appreciate you asking, but…" He fought the urge to take her hand, kissing the back while admitting that lately, the only person he needed in his life was her. And Chip, but he was only a fraction of a person. But Gideon couldn't admit any of that, because he didn't really feel any of that. All of this togetherness and goodwill was an illusion brought on by the holidays. If he thought he and Jane might stand a chance at sharing a real future, it was only because he was blinded by Santa goggles.

Chip cooed in his seat, wide-eyed, staring out the window at passing scenery as if he were a visitor on Mars.

In this moment, life was good.

Gideon wished for the power to freeze-frame time. He hated the pressure of knowing all of this could be yanked out from under him at any time. But maybe that knowledge was what made it so alluring?

The rest of the forty-minute ride was made in silence save for the baby cooing and the hypnotic drone of the windshield wipers when it started to rain.

Jane had fallen asleep, resting her head on his shoulder.

The fact that she trusted him to that extent made Gideon feel like a king. Lord knew he didn't deserve her trust. He'd sniped and barked at her from the moment they'd met. Constantly reminding her that he felt zero for her when nothing could be further from the truth.

For whatever time they had left together, he'd do better.

This would be the best Christmas she'd ever had.

He couldn't buy her a car or jewels, but he could give her—at least temporarily—the stability and companionship she claimed to need.

"WELL? WHAT DO you think?" A week later, after a busy morning filled with a successful well-child appointment for Chip and a postdelivery checkup for herself, Jane was finally back to her newfound passion— baking. Her heart raced and her palms sweated while waiting for Gideon to take his first bite of the chocolate chip cookie she'd modified from the original recipe. For whatever reason, his opinion mattered. "I added more vanilla—and played with the sugar ratio. There's more brown than white."

From his seat on the sofa, he clutched his chest, making a strangling sound.

Chip gummed a rubber pony in his carrier.

"Gideon? Are they that bad?"

He stopped fooling around to gift her with a giant smile. "They're *that* good. Holy crap, you could sell these things. They're amazing." He finished half the first dozen in one sitting. "You are making more, right?"

"Yes, but I was going to fill a tin for Mrs. Gentry."

"No. Give her the next batch. These are all mine." And he wasn't kidding. "Seriously, Jane. I'm blown away."

"Thank you." Her cheeks superheated under his praise.

"You're welcome. Now, get busy and make more—please."

While Gideon went out to work with Jelly Bean, Jane happily baked her afternoon away, and when the cabin smelled of sugar and flour and vanilla, and the counter had been covered with filled tins for friends and neighbors, she felt ready to burst with happiness. One answer about her past had been answered—she loved to bake.

Now, however, it was time to switch gears to decorating.

After popping a big batch of popcorn, she transferred Chip from his windup swing to his carrier, to "help" her make popcorn and cranberry strings for the tree. At first, the process was tricky, and the popcorn kept breaking before she could get it past the needle to slide onto the fishing line, but once she got the hang of it, it was fun.

She had about three feet completed when Gideon entered along with a gust of cold wind. The top of his black cowboy hat was covered in white, as were the shoulders of his long duster coat.

"I take it the rain turned to snow?" she teased.

"And then some." Once he'd hung his hat and coat on the rack by the door and stomped snow from his boots, he added a couple logs to the crackling fire, then joined her and Chip at the kitchen table. "Any cookies left?"

"About ten dozen."

"You're an angel." He zoned in on the oatmeal with butterscotch and toffee. Eyes closed, his groan was R-rated. "Are you kidding me?"

"Good?" Happiness bubbled through her like champagne. Had she always gotten this much joy from pleasing others through her baking?

"I know my baked goods—cakes, pastries, cinnamon rolls—and nothing, and I mean, *nothing* has ever tasted this good."

We have another winner on our hands. Product testing went through the roof.

Jane winced. It took a moment to regain her balance. Her head pounded, and time felt as if it had gone missing.

"What did you remember?" Gideon dropped his cookie on the counter to sit in the chair beside her.

"I'm not sure." She shook her head. "It was weird. Business-oriented. Not at all like me. It was probably nothing."

He shrugged. "My own two cents? These are good enough for you to sell. Sherrie's always holding bake sales. If you're still around after the holidays, I'm sure she'd appreciate you lending a hand."

"You think?"

He shoveled in two more cookies. "It's a no-brainer. You were born to bake."

She glowed under his praise.

Maybe after she put Chip to bed, she should look up tips on how to open a bakery on Pinterest? She didn't remember seeing one in Pine Glade.

For the next two hours, while watching the snow and laughing at Gideon's old Navy stories, Jane strung popcorn and cranberry chains for the tree while Chip inspected the reindeer on his green socks. Bliss didn't come close to describing her level of contentment. All along, could this have been the universe's kooky plan? Gideon had stopped being just a man, but her home.

Could I love him?

Love was an awfully strong word. But judging by the butterflies taking flight in her stomach every time he was near, or held her son, she might be well on her way to love. Which made no sense. A large majority of the time, he was cranky or snappy. But then those other times, like when he had made a rock bathing pool for her baby boy or bought her a Baby's 1st Christmas ornament or let her have his big comfy bed that smelled of him…

Swoon.

Pain crowned her head, squeezing with enough force to make her hold her breath and close her eyes. *I love you*, a mystery voice said. It sounded like her, but wasn't. *Never in a million years did I dream my life could be this complete.* In her mind's eye, was a flash of a sonogram. Of a man's hand pressed to a flat, sunkissed belly. Hers?

What was happening? Could she be married? How? How could she feel as if her sun and moon rose over Gideon if somewhere out there was another man she supposedly loved? It made no sense. Especially since she felt no connection whatsoever to her former life.

"While waiting for Jelly Bean to decide if she was going to cooperate today," Gideon said, oblivious to the quiet war raging in her head, "I remembered a fun thing I did for Christmas back in elementary school. You'll probably think it's stupid, but—"

"Tell me." *Please. Make me focus on anything but this nightmarish confusion.* She finished off her current string with a knot, then draped it around the tree. It looked quintessentially country Christmas, but she still had a long way to go to cover the whole fir.

"Okay, so I remember we used this stuff called salt dough clay to make a snowball shape. Then, when we weren't throwing them at each other, we mashed them by making impressions with our handprints. Once they dried, we painted them and gave them to our parents."

"Oh, that's adorable. I'll bet your mom loved it." *I love the way even your simplest story draws me out of my fear and makes me feel connected and whole, if only for a moment.*

He snorted. "By then, she'd already taken off. Dad patted me on the back and told me I did a good job. Then he used it for an ashtray."

Eyes stinging from barely restrained tears, Jane covered her gaping mouth with her hands. "That's terrible."

"It is what it is." Gideon was still thankfully oblivious to her struggle. With luck, she'd keep him that way.

"I'm looking up the recipe right now. Let's make them for our tree. They'll be darling keepsakes for Chip."

"Agreed. But he's a guy, Jane. Let's try to refrain from descriptive words like *darling*."

"Good thinking." After sniffing back tears, she forced a laugh while grabbing the iPad from its charger. In under a minute, she'd found the recipe and dozens of adorable photos of goopy-handed infants and kids showing off their ornaments. "We can so do this," she said, already grabbing flour from the pantry.

"Wait—you want me to make one, too?"

"Duh. We're making a family Christmas tree."

"But we're not a family."

He couldn't have hurt her worse with a physical blow. "Maybe not in the traditional sense, but we sort of are."

Gideon took forever to let that sink in. Once he did, his long, indecipherable exhale hurt even more. But then her heart fluttered when he nodded. "You know, you're right. I suppose we kind of are a family. Temporary. But good."

"See? And all the best families make ornaments together. If we're going to try this, we might as well be the best."

"Just like that?"

"I'm not saying it will be easy, but it's certainly worth the effort, don't you think?" *Because if I have any more visions like that last one, I'll need backup. I'll need to know that whatever happens to my future self, my current self has a true friend.*

"What I think is that you're more than a little crazy, but I like it. Let's start making ornaments."

After prepping the dough, Jane moved her popcorn-and cranberry-garland-making supplies and got both boys set up at the table, which she'd covered with long sheets of wax paper.

Watching Gideon focus on making the perfect ball, which he then flattened with the bottom of a coffee cup before pressing Chip's fingers into the surface, was the cutest thing Jane had ever seen. He may not like to admit it, but Gideon was ideal father material.

"Will this do?" Gideon asked of his finished product. He still held Chip securely in the crook of his arm.

"It's perfect. The directions said to use a toothpick to add a hole for ribbon. I'll do that."

"Cool. Thanks."

"Make one for you," she urged.

"Only if you make one, too."

"Deal." She brought the whole box of toothpicks to the table, then grabbed a hunk of clay.

"Think we could make other shapes, too?"

"I don't know why not. What do you have in mind?"

"If you lend me your cookie cutters," he said, "I'll make Santa and his reindeer. And elves. Lots of elves."

"Better watch out," she said from the sink while washing her hands. "If I didn't know better, I'd say you're enjoying yourself."

He chuckled. "I've spent nights doing worse things."

"Tell me."

His smile faded. "Really?"

Swallowing hard, she nodded. *I want to know everything about you—the good and bad.*

She remained silent for a long time. The only sound was a cold, shrill wind rattling the windows. Inside, the fire merrily crackled, lending the room a warm golden glow. But Gideon's expression had turned dark.

After what felt like forever, he sighed. "The most recent thing would have to be the night Missy passed. I'd been watching a ball game—don't even remember who was playing, but I got a knock on my door. It was a police officer. I was still living in San Diego at the time. He asked me a few questions, and then just came right out with it—said Missy had been killed and asked me to ID her remains."

"Oh no…" Her heart ached for him.

"Took me ten hours to drive to the morgue. She was bloody and bruised. Her skin w-was waxy gray." He choked on the words, absentmindedly stroking Chip's downy hair. "The last time we spoke was ugly. We both said things I'm now ashamed of, but—"

"It's okay." Jane rose to hug Gideon from behind. "I mean, of course, it's not. Nothing about that story is *okay*, but people say horrible things to each other all the time. Usually we get a second chance to make things right, but you didn't. I'm so sorry."

"You shouldn't be. It has nothing to do with you. And

anyway…" He hardened beneath her touch, then stood, passing her the baby. "What makes you a relationship expert when you don't even know your own name?"

His cruel words hit her like a slap.

And then he was heading for the door.

"Where are you going?" He couldn't leave. Not like this.

What do you mean, you're leaving me? We're married. I'm having your baby…

Pain drove Jane to her knees.

The intensity was so great, she struggled to not to drop her son.

"Jane!" Gideon knelt by her side. "What's wrong? Can you hear me?"

She nodded.

He slid his arms beneath her, grunting to stand, but carried her and Chip to the sofa. "What happened?"

"I-I don't know." *Liar.* "One second I felt fine, and the next I had a killer headache." At least that much was true.

"How are you now?"

"Fine." Except for her bruised ego. All in one night, she'd told an imaginary man in her head she loved him, and then he apparently left her, and now Gideon was on the verge of leaving, too? It was all too much. She wanted to tell him about all of it, but couldn't. What if he thought she was crazy?

What if I am crazy?

Chapter Fourteen

Two nights before Christmas, with a belly full of Jane's latest cookies, Gideon was back at the kitchen table with Chip on his lap. He was painting one of his home-made elf ornaments and digging it. Geez, if any of his old SEAL teammates found out about this, they'd have him shipped off for medical testing.

But life with Jane and her son was good. Real good.

Was there such a thing as too good?

Probably. But for now, he didn't care. Granted, she had her headache spells, after which she weirded out, but that was understandable, right? Because of the pain?

For once in his life, he couldn't bear doing what he *should*. Instead, he'd been opting for what he wanted. Knowing he could never fully commit to Jane and her son, did that make him a bad person not cutting things off? Absolutely. But he wasn't sure what to do about it.

How did he quit her?

Maybe after the holidays he'd find a way, but not now. He couldn't do it. And so he kept painting, and jiggling the baby, and wishing he cared as much about finding his next horse client as he did making Jane happy.

"I've got an idea," he said midway through paint-ing his third elf.

"Let's hear it."

"What if I backed you in a bakery?"

"That's crazy." She pulled red velvet hanging ribbon through one of Chip's tiny hand ornaments that they'd painted the previous night. "I'd never let you do something risky like that."

"What if I didn't give you a choice? Those cookies of yours are phenomenal. Maybe I think the fine folks of Pine Glade deserve to eat them every day of their lives."

"Please don't tease." She snipped the end of her ribbon and tied it into a bow. "Not about this. I can't explain, but…" She pressed her hand to her chest. "The dream feels too dear. Too fragile. Having a bakery of my own would be…" Her eyes welled. "It would be a dream come true."

"Then let me help you." He leaned forward too abruptly, startling Chip into a full wail. He clutched the infant close, rocking him, whispering *shhh* into his tiny ear.

"Why?"

"I'm getting older. I've been looking for an investment. I need something to do that's less physical."

"You're lying."

"Why would I lie?"

"I don't know. Maybe you feel sorry for me or just want me out of your hair bad enough that you're willing to finance my exit? Who knows? There could be any number of rational reasons."

"Okay, since we're laying our cards out on the table, what if I'm making this offer not just because I believe in your product, but I believe in you? I like you. I trust you not to let me down."

She dried her eyes with a paper towel. Sniffled.

"What if we get knee-deep into this business, then my family is found?"

"We'll cross that bridge when we come to it."

"You're serious?"

He held out his free hand for her to shake.

"Let's do it." She smiled through tears, clasping his hand, but then abandoning their platonic shake for a hug that landed her on his lap, tossing her arms around his neck.

With the baby sandwiched between them, time slowed to the point that maybe Gideon was no longer sure of his own identity. Jane smelled insanely good. Clean and soapy and not anything like him. She was fresh. Whole. Her purity attracted him like a gravitational pull. She was the sun and he a lowly planet, spinning under her spell.

Unlike Missy, she didn't lie. She didn't pretend everything between them was okay when nothing could be further from the truth. At first, when he'd arrived home minus his leg, Missy had been supportive for the local news pieces about the wounded warrior. But when the camera lights went off, and she grasped the enormity of her new life with a cripple, everything that used to be good between them unraveled. Like a curtain being drawn back on a story playing out onstage, he learned that if he was no longer a hotshot SEAL, she no longer wanted to be with him. Her life hadn't been centered around them, per se, but the whole SEAL culture. Her friendships with fellow SEAL wives. She'd parlayed the cachet of being married to a SEAL into a promotion. She'd never understood the fact that he wasn't a SEAL because it was cool, but because good people needed help. When they couldn't be strong, he and his team could.

"Let's get started on our bakery in the morning," Gideon said into Jane's ear, fighting a primal urge to sweep his lips along her jawline and neck. Across her collarbone, the mound of her breasts. He shifted, needing her closer.

She complied, molding herself to him, to the baby, to the infant that if Gideon would just let go, might someday grow into his child. But did he have the courage? Did he dare put himself up for Jane's judgment? What if he abandoned himself to her only to have her laugh in his face?

Me? Spend the rest of my life with a one-legged man? The idea was too cruel.

He shifted Jane off of his lap and back to her seat, inadvertently knocking the baby's carrier. Chip woke with a vengeance, crying so hard that Gideon worried he couldn't breathe.

"I'm sure he's hungry." Jane took him, in the process brushing their arms. Did she feel the tension? Did she crave him like he craved her?

I hope not. I would never want her to be in this much pain.

"THERE ARE TWO commercial properties available," Amelia Lincoln with Homefront Realty said the next afternoon from behind her office desk. The room was pleasant enough. Striped wallpaper, blue carpet and a conference table large enough for eight. But none of that mattered when all Jane could think about was how much gratitude she owed the man beside her.

And how much she struggled with the gut feeling that this was a horrible decision. Gideon barely knew her. She barely knew herself. If she was a good person, she'd put a stop to this now—before it went further.

Mrs. Gentry had volunteered to stay with Chip. Jane had pumped enough milk to last through the evening feeding.

She should have been excited, but nausea churned her belly. Her pulse hammered and her palms were sweating.

"Here, and here." Amelia pointed to squares on a map that were on the opposite ends of the boardwalk. "Now, they're both an adequate size for a bakery installation, but this one—" she touched the square nearest the toy store "—already has a commercial kitchen. It would need fine-tuning, but basically, the working parts are all there. I'd say with minimal redecorating, you could be in business in just over a month."

"We'll take it." Gideon cupped Jane's hand, giving her a squeeze. She wrestled back tears.

"B-but you haven't even seen it." How could he be so pumped about this decision when she knew it was wrong?

"Don't need to." Gideon smiled. "You said yourself this is the best of only a couple options."

"Wonderful," the Realtor said. "You two stay put. I'll draw up the papers."

Once Amelia left them alone, closing her office door, Jane turned to Gideon. "You don't have to do this. Granted, it's a lovely dream, but ultimately, too much. You hardly know me." She swallowed the lump lurking at the back of her throat. "Correction—you literally don't know me. This is lunacy. Putting what has to be a huge chunk of your savings behind a woman you don't—"

"Shh…" He cupped her face in his big hands. Their chairs were close enough that all he'd have to do to kiss her would be to make a slight lean to the left.

Kiss me! her soul cried. *What are you waiting for?* That was the kind of commitment she really wanted. One that at least emotionally promised they were on the same relationship page.

His gaze searched hers, and with them both breathing heavy, he brushed her lower lip with his thumb. The touch was brief, wholly innocent, yet never in her life had she felt anything more erotic.

"I'm doing this," he said, "because I trust you. And because no matter what becomes of your future, I want you to know I have your back. Always. No matter what, you and your son will not only have this business to lean on, but me. I promise."

"Thank you. But if you feel that way, why can't we—"

"We're all set." Amelia burst into the room. "This was such a nice surprise. Usually, right before the holidays we're dead. But you picked a wonderful time to get started. January might be slow, but with Valentine's Day, you'll have more business than you can shake a stick at." She thrust a pile of papers across her desk, along with a pen. "Gideon, if you'll sign everywhere I've flagged, as soon as I get a copy of your ID and the deposit and first and last month's rent, I'll get you the keys."

Jane nodded, but then said, "If you don't mind, could you please give us a moment alone?"

Amelia's bright smile faded. "Of course. Is anything wrong?"

Everything. But none of which she could tell this Realtor or Gideon.

"What's up?" he asked once she'd gone.

Angling sideways in her chair, Jane forced a deep breath. "I don't want to do this." *I can't live with the liability of not knowing who I am hanging over my head.*

I can't hurt you financially and emotionally when my memory does return.

"What do you mean? I thought it was settled?"

She shook her head. "It was a lovely dream—and maybe someday we'll make it a reality. But for now, let's maybe try selling packets of my cookies to other shops. We'll use them as a test market."

His gaze narrowed. "What do you know about test markets?"

"Nothing?" She forced a laugh. "The phrase just popped into my head." Could it be another memory? Was it wrong that she didn't want to know?

A knock sounded on the door. Amelia walked in. "I totally understand if you have cold feet, so I contacted the building's owner. Since you two are locals, she said it would be all right for me to give you the keys—just so you could take a peek. This would never happen in a big city—a Realtor letting you take a peek on your own—but around here, we love to give our clients that personal touch."

"Thank you," Jane said, "but we couldn't."

Gideon took the keys. "Let's check it out. What could it hurt?"

"Exactly." Amelia's smile returned.

When Jane and Gideon left the office, a light snow fell, covering the picturesque town in what looked like fantastical powdered sugar. She should have been ecstatic, but her heart beat heavy with dread.

This is it. You did it.

Jane had heard enough of the voices in her head to recognize the man again, but this time, she'd caught a softer side. Happier. What had she done? In this moment, it didn't matter. She had to find the courage to tell Gideon the truth—that more and more slivers of her memory were returning. But when should she tell him? How?

It was a short walk to the shop. Just down from Santa's park, right in the thick of the most crowded section of the boardwalk, her fantasy bakery sat between the toy store and a T-shirt shop. In the summers, she'd put comfy benches outside for any shoppers who needed a cookie break. Overflowing pots of lobelia, petunias and snapdragons.

"Here we are." Gideon stopped before the only vacant storefront on that side of the street. "If we do rent it, what are you going to call it?"

"I don't know," she said. Tell him. *Now. Only then will he understand why going into business together is an awful idea.*

"You'd better start thinking about it," he said upon opening the door. "A great name is important."

"I'm sure…"

She walked inside with a slow reverence, scarcely able to breathe. The wood floors were dusty, the service counter in need of a scrub, but the place had a happy feel. Loved. Amelia had told them that for years it had been a diner, but the owner had retired and with no family wanting to step up and take over, she'd liquidated her physical assets and closed for good.

It's gone. Get over it. Console yourself with the money.

Go away, she longed to shout at the man in her head. He was mean again, and she wanted him gone. She hated him for intruding upon this sacred place.

Towering plate-glass windows covered the front, with adorable display cases on either side of the centered door. The ceiling was at least fifteen feet tall, and made her feel as if she were flying. Like some of the old-fashioned pharmacies she'd been in, there was a balcony.

Dust motes danced in slanted sunbeams.

"What's up there?" she whispered.

"Probably offices?" he whispered back. "Maybe an efficiency apartment where you and Chip could live? Why are we whispering?"

"No clue." She giggled again. "This place feels sacred to me—like a church."

He wrapped his arms around her from behind, resting his chin atop her head. "Happy?"

I could be. With you. If only these voices would leave my head. "I want to be happy, but taking on a business is too big of a liability. It's a bad idea."

"You know what's a really bad idea? Depriving the world of your cookies." She could have purred when he kissed the crown of her head. His touch was so gentle, maybe she'd imagined it, but she needed it to be real. "Besides, don't forget I'd get a chunk of the profits. Considering how packed this street is on any given summer day, we'll both be rich."

"From your lips to God's ears." Only she already was rich —immeasurably so, for having Gideon in her life. "But I still don't want it. Maybe someday, but not now. Please understand."

Spinning her to face him, they locked stares. "You're sure?"

Heart pounding, she nodded.

"For the record, I think this is a mistake, but I understand. Guess we'd better lock up and tell Amelia you've decided to ruin her Christmas."

"Gideon…" Jane frowned.

"Just kidding." He nudged her shoulder with his. "I

get it. And hell, I'm nuts for thinking it would work. But it was fun to think about, wasn't it?"

Swallowing back tears, she said, "It sure was."

"You did what?"

Gideon bumped into West on his way out of Kingman's. He'd been arresting a shoplifter, but had sent him off to the jail with a deputy.

"Almost rented Jane a bakery, but we backed out at the last minute. Now she's waiting on the paint she picked out for the baby's makeshift closet nursery to get shaken. I would be loading our lumber for his shelves if I weren't yakking with you." The nursery project was a consolation prize.

"Gideon..." West removed his sheriff's hat, using his shirtsleeve to wipe his brow. "Slow down. Have you thought any of this through? You don't even know this woman's real name. What if she's a con artist, and you're playing right into her hands?"

Gideon hardened his jaw, squeezing his hands into fists. "If we hadn't been friends for fifteen years, I'd punch you into the next county. Jane's a good woman. The best."

"Maybe so. But thank the good Lord you didn't do something as drastic as jumping into business with her." Shaking his head, he said, "Hell, next you're going to tell me you're marrying the gal."

"Never. You know after what went down with Missy I'll never marry again."

"But you actually considered sinking a ton of money into a woman you don't know?"

"That was different."

"Bull. Because we've known each other practically since we were kids, would you please just be careful?

Don't give Jane direct access to any accounts. My job is dealing with scum of the earth. Folks around here like to think we're protected from seedier elements, but bad things happen in small towns, too. All the time. Think about it."

"Screw you."

West tipped his hat and walked away.

"Oh—and you and the mayor are uninvited for Christmas dinner!"

West flipped him a backhanded bird.

Gideon drove the truck around to the lumber side of the store, got his supplies loaded, then returned to the front to find Jane waiting. The clouds had passed, and she stood with her hands on the shopping cart handle.

She'd tipped her face back to drink in the sun.

Beautiful didn't come close to describing her.

Her dark hair tumbled past her shoulders in luxurious waves. When he'd held her back in their would-be store, kissing the top of her head, breathing her in, he'd never wanted to let her go. She was changing him on a fundamental level. Getting him all messed up inside. The longer he was around her and her son, the more he connected with his old self. That man had wanted nothing more than a wife and kids and a house and dog and hamsters.

When Gideon lost his leg, he'd lost sight of that dream. Believed it an impossibility—just like he'd told West. But what if it wasn't? What if he changed his mind and took a chance on a better life? A shared life? What if maybe—just maybe—with a kindhearted woman like Jane, his missing leg wouldn't be an issue? If not—

"Let me in." Her knock on the truck's passenger-side window woke him from his daydream of never again being alone. Just as well. He'd never been much good at making dreams come true.

He pressed the auto-unlock button for her door, then hopped out to help her load their purchases into the bed.

West was wrong.

Since when had it become a bad thing to place trust in someone? Especially a woman like Jane. She might have lost her past, but her present was an open book. She was a great mom. A great help around his place. Every soul she encountered from the donkey and chickens to Mrs. Gentry and Sherrie instantly loved her.

Bottom line? Jane made him want to be a better man.

"Sorry I took so long." She fastened her seat belt while he drove them toward the cabin. "At the last minute, I changed my mind about the color. I went with pale green—it's happy and reminds me of the first leaves in spring. Is that okay?"

"Of course." *I want to take your hand in mine, raise it to my lips to kiss the back and then your palm, reassuring you that no matter what you decide, it will always be right for me.* But he didn't. Couldn't. So he did the next best thing—smiled in her direction and said, "It's going to look great. I have a hundred percent faith in your decisions."

"I wish you wouldn't say things like that."

"Why? It's the truth."

"Not really. Neither of us know my truth."

"Where is this coming from? Did you have another headache spell while you were in the store?"

"No." She did rub her forehead. "Sorry. It's been a long day, and I'm tired."

"Sure. I understand."

But he didn't. He was busting his balls trying to be nice to her; why wouldn't she let him?

He drove in silence for a few minutes, then said, "I ran into West while you were messing with paint."

"Was Sherrie with him? She is so sweet. I can't wait to see them both on Christmas. I'll bet her baby bump is getting huge."

He winced. "About that. He can't come."

"Oh no. Why?"

"Last-minute police thing." *Liar.* What else could he do? It would break her heart if he told her West believed her to be a first-rate con artist.

"What about Sherrie? She shouldn't spend the holiday alone."

"She's got a mayor thing. They'll be okay. You just worry about making sure you've got plenty of desserts to go with Mrs. Gentry's ham."

"You and your sweet tooth…" Her sideways smile erased what remained of West's ugly words.

"Speaking of which—can you make pies?"

"I don't know, but if you want to invest in a few more baking supplies, it would be easy enough to find out." Her smile, her wide-eyed optimism in the face of what would destroy most women in her place, all served as inspiration to Gideon. Her honesty and goodness were day by day making him a better person.

Screw West. He was an idiot.

Jane was Gideon's own personal heroine.

If his old friend so much as hinted at anything to the contrary again, Gideon would knock his lights out.

Chapter Fifteen

Three a.m. Christmas Eve, Jane should have been sleeping, but how could she close her eyes when everything she'd ever wanted could either come to fruition or implode around her? Granted, she had only been aware of wanting to launch a bakery and maybe even a lifetime commitment with Gideon for a short while, but time had stopped mattering.

That afternoon, they'd transformed Gideon's closet into a small nursery. They'd painted together and measured for shelves and comforted Chip when he'd been frightened by the power saw, and she'd realized that no matter what happened with her identity, this was where she wanted to be.

It was understandable that because of what had happened with his ex, Gideon would be skittish when it came to diving into a new relationship. But what he didn't realize was that they'd already done just that—and it was beautiful. The three of them together felt as if they had always been meant to be.

What about your memories? Especially the darker ones? Were those always meant to be?

Her heart pounded uncomfortably fast. Far too awake with dread over the inevitability of having to come clean with Gideon and share everything she'd been going through, Jane reached for his iPad from the nightstand.

Earlier, he'd asked if she made pies. No time like the present to find a couple recipes to wow him.

She opened her browser to a favorite cooking site when an ad popped up for a magazine subscription. Annoyed, she clicked it, but missed the *X*, and inadvertently opened a new site. An article heading caught her attention: Cookie Behemoth Ventures into Internet Sales.

The potential business owner in her was curious what becoming a cookie behemoth would entail, so she clicked on the article:

> *When it went public minus its beloved CEO and founder, Allison Ford, critics in the food industry predicted overbaked sales accompanied by sour milk for cookie behemoth Sugar Rush. After a hostile takeover ousted Ms. Ford, many of her longtime employees staged walkouts in protest of her forced exit. However, under the new direction of Deacon Montgomery's global vision, internet sales have profits soaring. Stockholders can't get enough of this company's cookies or shares.*

Jane closed her eyes to a blinding headache. She braced herself for the memory sure to follow.

It's done. Bow out gracefully. All you'll do by fighting is hurt yourself. I'm sorry it had to be this way, but you refused to listen to reason. Taking the company public has made you a very wealthy woman.

With hands trembling to the point that it was a struggle to type the words *Sugar Rush* and *Allison Ford* into the iPad's search feature, Jane held her breath while awaiting the results. She clicked to see images, then froze.

Pulse beating fast enough to be scary, she dropped the iPad to the bed, pressing her hands over her runaway heart.

No, no, no...

She knew one day her past would come back to claim her, but not like this. She'd planned to ease into it with Gideon beside her.

The woman gazing back at her from dozens of postage stamp–size images was her. Allison Ford was *her*. But at the same time, *not*.

She needed to wake Gideon. Tell him what she'd learned.

Tossing back the covers, she pressed her feet to the floor. Cold hardwood chilled her soles, giving her momentary pause.

Wait, her heart pounded over and over again.

She squeezed her eyes tight, willing memories away, but behind her eyelids, lights flashed as if she were riding with the top down on a sweltering summer day. Faster and faster she caught glimpses of herself with a chiseled-featured man. There was romance and flowers. Business advice. Decadent trips and lavish promises.

I'm pregnant. I'm carrying your son. How can you leave me? Us? I love you.

It had all been a game. An elaborate ruse. He'd taken her company and her heart. The day she'd run off to the woods had been the day their divorce became final— although the marriage had ended long before. She loved the woods. There were even articles about it:

CEO Allison Ford completes the Appalachian Trail. Says she'd do it again, but only if she packs an extra supply of cookies.

Hands pressed to her temples, Jane remembered feeling so alone on the day she'd vanished. Ripped from family and friends. Deacon had alienated her from everyone she'd ever loved. Or had she done that herself? Much had grown clear, yet other parts of herself seemed as out of reach as a distant fog.

Go to Gideon. Tell him everything. Let him help.

No. Once he learned she hadn't been honest with him about her returning memory, he might ask her to leave. He'd tell her to go home, back to her "real" life.

And what about her plan to sell packets of cookies out of other shop owners' stores?

But then how silly was that? She'd owned the largest cookie company in the world. Larger than Mrs. Fields. Compared to what she'd spent most of her life building, this new venture was laughable. But it was also real. A tangible display of the way Gideon made her feel— smart and capable and as far from being a failure as she'd ever dreamed possible. Of course, she probably owned her own house somewhere, but without Gideon there to share it, it would never be a true home.

So far, all she'd learned about her past was that everything she'd held dear had been ripped away. She wasn't ready to have that happen again should she lose Gideon.

Having no crystal ball, there was no way to tell how he would react to the news that practically from the day she'd moved in, snippets of her memory had been returning. Now she knew even more pieces to her own personal puzzle, but she still didn't have them all. Which was why she'd wait.

Honestly? She had no other choice.

Sure you do. Be honest. For all the man has done for you, he deserves that much.

Yes, he did. But selfishly, for her own sanity, she couldn't yet take the chance that her truth may prove to be their end.

"WOMAN, ARE YOU trying to fatten me like a Christmas turkey?" Gideon sat up on the sofa, awakened by the tantalizing scent of pancakes and bacon and coffee.

"Maybe." She left the kitchen island to deliver a breakfast fit more for an emperor than a king. There were also fat link sausages, strawberries carved into roses, and a giant slice of poppy seed bread.

"How long have you been up?"

"Not long. Chip was hungry, so I figured I might as well feed us, too."

"I'm not complaining. Thanks, buddy," he said to the infant who was already drooling in his windup swing. After eating a healthy portion of his meal, Gideon asked, "What are our plans for today? I've got caulking to do on Little Man's shelves. Do you want to help or prep for tomorrow?"

"As lovely as that caulking offer sounds," she said from the sink, "I've got a ton of baking to do. Oh— and I found a recipe for a caramel apple pie that I think you'll devour."

He groaned in happiness. "You are my own Christmas miracle."

"Likewise." Her blown kiss affected him almost as deeply as the real thing. Had things been different between them, he'd have stepped up behind her, sweeping her long hair from her neck, kissing the skin he'd bared only to continue a slow trail to her lips. "I figure our first order of business should be prepping the barn. And before I forget, would you mind giving me Sherrie's number? I wanted to check in—make sure she has plans. How sad would it be for her to spend the holidays alone?"

Guilt assailed him for not having told Jane the truth about what had gone down in front of Kingman's. But he stood by his decision to keep West's concerns to himself. What his old friend didn't understand was just how much Jane had come to mean to Gideon. What they'd been through on that trail bonded them in a way few other couples ever would be.

It had been a gift he would forever cherish.

His gift to her would be calling West and eating crow. Downright begging if he had to for him and Sherrie to show up for this elaborate dinner Jane and Mrs. Gentry had planned.

"Gideon?" Jane asked. "Did you hear me? I need Sherrie's number."

"No. I mean, you can have it, but let me call West. His schedule changes on a dime. Maybe he'll be able to get away after all?"

"You think?" Her smile unraveled him, stole more and more of his resolve to keep a safe distance. "That would be great. Thank you." She abandoned dishwashing to kiss his cheek.

"You're welcome." It took far too much willpower not to turn his head, forcing their lips to collide. "What can I do to help?"

"Since you asked…" She batted her eyelashes and grinned. "I'd be awfully appreciative if you set up sawhorses in the barn, then place a few of those planks leaning in the northeast corner over them for us to use as a table. After that, please turn on the stall warmers so that by tomorrow around two p.m., it's nice and toasty."

"Remind me again why we're eating in the barn when we have a perfectly fine house?"

"I saw it on Pinterest."

"What's that? A magazine?"

"You've never heard of Pinterest? Scoot over."

The baby's swing had wound down, and Chip kicked up a fuss. She got him started again before retrieving the iPad from the kitchen counter, then joining Gideon on the sofa.

She sat beside him. Far too close for him to think about anything other than how irresponsible it would be to slip his arm around her waist, tugging her onto his lap. While she pulled up what was apparently a digital picture book for grown-ups, he failed miserably at trying not to catch whiffs of her hair.

"Look." She pointed at a series of gussied-up barns, all decked out in flowers—flower garlands and fancy flower arrangements. Vintage milk cans filled with wildflowers. In every photo, elaborate table settings ruled. Three stacked plates in varying sizes and colors per person and more wineglasses than the town of Pine Glade had bottles of wine. Lace tablecloths and more flowers gracing the center in Ball jar vases. "Aren't they pretty?"

"You do realize these are staged? No one's barn actually looks like this—especially not in the middle of winter."

"Then I guess we'll be starting a new trend. It's going to be fab—" She pointed to his feet. "You slept in your boots again?"

"Occupational hazard."

"Nut job is more like it. When is this last time you had them off?"

"Not that it's any of your business, but last night in the shower." He hadn't dared soak in his bath since she'd been there. The bathroom door lock was broken.

The risk of her walking in on him—however slim—was too great.

"Whatever. I suppose if you get your appointed tasks done in time for me to measure for a tablecloth, I won't give you grief."

"Mighty kind of you, ma'am. If I had my hat on, I'd tip it."

She laughed. "Wish you did have it on. Might hide your hat head."

"I don't have hat head."

"Look in the mirror much?"

He scrambled up to do just that. She was right.

"Told you so." She'd sneaked up behind him, and they now shared the bathroom mirror. "Not that I'm complaining. You're still an all right–looking guy."

"All right?" They bantered with each other's reflections. It somehow felt more intimate. The sort of thing a couple might do while brushing their teeth before bed.

"Maybe a smidge better than average. But I wouldn't go higher than that." The spark in her eyes and hitch in her breath told him she was lying. That she was as hot for him as he was her. But even if she hadn't just had a baby, the sight of his missing leg would be a mood killer.

"Fair enough." He caught and held her gaze in the mirror.

She licked her lips. Raised her chin. "You ever planning on kissing me?"

"Nope." Neither had broken their stare. The intimacy of it might kill him, but he physically couldn't look away.

"Why?"

"Already told you. I've been with one woman and she was more than enough to make me swear off the fairer sex for life. No offense to you, but…" He broke his stare to grip the counter's cool granite edge. He was a bastard for lying to her, so he added a soul-crushing line of truth. "I'm just not built the way I used to be."

"What does that mean? You're making up excuses. Your only problem is fear of commitment. You're afraid of getting hurt again. Newsflash—aren't we all? You think I'm not terrified of—"

"What could you possibly have to fear? You don't know what it's like to have a broken—"

"A broken heart? You're wrong."

Gaze narrowed, he asked, "Did you have more memories?"

"No." She didn't meet his stare. Could she be lying? "I just wised up enough to realize that if I were madly in love with Chip's biological father, odds are he would have moved heaven and hell to find me. May or may not have come to your attention, but no one in my former life gives a damn. I'm on my own. And for the record? It does hurt. But that doesn't mean I'm willing give up on life—or love."

"You don't love me."

"I could." There she went again with her stubborn chin.

Chip cried out.

"Want me to get him?" Gideon asked, desperate to escape her and this conversation.

"Sure. Thanks."

He left her there, alone in the bathroom with her big green eyes threatening to storm. Everyone knew green clouds were the worst, but he didn't care. Couldn't. Because that would imply a level of intimacy that might drive him over the edge.

"Sweetie, Mommy's in trouble…" Later that morning, while Gideon worked with Jelly Bean, Jane fed her son on the sofa. The Christmas tree lights glowed, the branches laden with homemade ornaments, each one rich with meaning. Before leaving, Gideon had made sure a toasty fire crackled in the hearth. The air smelled of cinnamon from her latest batch of oatmeal cookies. All in the cabin was exactly as it should be on Christmas Eve, yet nothing could be more of a mess. "We lead pretty sweet lives here, yet if Daddy Gideon finds out we have our own house in Phoenix, he'll probably ask us to leave."

Her throat ached with unshed tears, but there was no use crying over matters she couldn't fix.

Gazing at her child, her heart swelled with love. With her pinkie finger, she traced his eyebrows, nose and cheeks. In all her life, she'd never created anything more perfect. But day by day, the bond she'd forged with Gideon grew closer.

How did she break down his walls? Why was he so afraid?

The door opened and there he was. He shut it against the draft. Usually when she fed Chip, Gideon looked away. Made a smart-ass joke. This time he stood transfixed.

"Sorry about earlier," she finally said, unable to bear the heavy silence. "But I'm not apologizing about confessing how I feel. I don't want to be your friend."

He bowed his head.

Desperation spurred her forward. "You can't deny that we're good together."

"We've known each other barely over three weeks."

"From my perspective, that's a lifetime."

"We keep going in circles, Jane. You'll never change my mind."

"Tell me you feel nothing for me beyond friendship."

"I don't."

"Tell me while looking into my eyes."

He couldn't.

"Thank you for proving my point."

"All I proved, Jane, is that I'm tired of this conversation."

"Then ask me to stay." Panic laced her words. "You don't have to marry me, just tell me you want me to stay. I can't be alone." From what little she'd learned about her former self, everything she'd once loved in her life was gone.

"We'll find you a nice little place in town. You and Chip will be comfortable. You'll make lots of friends."

"It won't be the same. And if you want us gone so bad, why did you just transform your closet into a nursery?"

"Call it temporary insanity. Why are you afraid of being alone? What happened to you that would make you think my company is preferable to your own?"

She remained silent. Just like that part of her life that led to her giving everything she had to Deacon. She hadn't wanted to be alone then, either. What she'd felt for him hadn't been love, but desperation. A little girl crying out for her family not to leave her.

A strangled gasp escaped her.

That was it. They were gone.

A sailboat flashed before her mind's eye. At first, there was happiness, and many lessons. Hoist the sail. Retie that knot. Then there was thunder and lightning and waves so tall that when their boat dipped between the swells, they couldn't see over the tops. *Cape Hat-*

teras Coast Guard, this is the sailing vessel Mist. *We are taking on water and in need of immediate assistance. We have four souls aboard.* Her mother, father and big brother drowned. She alone survived the night, clinging to the side of the hull. Just like Gideon, she was alone in the world. But if they united, that all would change. They could be a family. Why couldn't he see?

Tell him your whole story. How you were raised by your grandmother, but now, even she's gone. Make him understand.

Sounded good in theory, but what if Gideon felt like she was trying to substitute him for her family, her husband? What if he accused her of not truly having feelings for him, but of trying to mask feelings of her own?

Are you?

The question slapped her back to reality. To the fact that Gideon knelt before her, cupping her cheek, wiping silent tears from her cheek with the pad of his thumb. "What are you remembering, Jane? Let me in."

"It's nothing." She sniffed back tears. The baby had eaten his fill, so she shifted him, with shaking fingers, fastening her nursing bra and blouse. "How are things going in the barn?"

"Fine." His gaze narrowed. "West and Sherrie will be here for dinner."

"Wonderful. Thank you for calling."

"What aren't you telling me?" He searched her face.

"It's Christmas Eve." She squared her shoulders and forced a smile. "Let's be happy."

If only it were that simple...

Chapter Sixteen

Christmas morning, while Jane and the baby were still sleeping, Gideon made fast work of feeding Jelly Bean, the chickens and the donkey. He turned the stall warmers higher, because Jane had asked him to have the barn nice and toasty for their party. He then fished a sack of presents from where he'd hidden it in the tack room.

The last time he'd celebrated a truly festive Christmas morning had been the year he and Missy were first married. He'd just returned from a nine-month stint in Syria. The hazardous duty pay allowed for a diamond tennis bracelet for her and the truck he was still driving today. She'd made and burned a turkey—not that it mattered, since later in the day they'd gone to her parents' for a big family dinner. To date, he'd considered it one of his happier memories.

Today, though, his chest felt near bursting from excitement with the anticipation of giving Jane and Chip their gifts.

Finished in the barn, he hustled back to the cabin.

His plan was to turn on the tree lights, arrange the already-wrapped gifts under it, then stoke the fire until it filled the cabin with warmth and a merry crackle. From there, he'd whip up some bacon and scrambled eggs. Oh—and carols. He'd have to find holiday music on his satellite radio.

He mounted the porch stairs, taking them two at a time, excited about enacting his plan, but when he opened the door, all-out chaos ruled.

Chip wailed.

Jane looked like a crazy woman. Her hair was powdered with what looked like flour, as was Chip's entire face. She held him in front of the sink, wiping a washcloth over his eyes.

In protector mode, Gideon flung their gifts to the sofa, then charged to help. "What happened?"

Tear streaks ran through the flour on her face.

"I was making pancakes when I accidentally turned the beaters on high. I was holding the baby when a cloud erupted. I think flour must've gotten in his eyes."

"Probably." Gideon took the baby and cloth. "But you're going to be just fine, aren't you, little man?"

Red-eyed, Chip huffed.

Once he'd finished cleaning the baby's face, Gideon rinsed the cloth and worked on Momma.

"I feel so bad," she said.

"It was an accident. Could've happened to anyone."

"I guess. But I'm the one making my baby scream on Christmas morning."

"True." He winked before pulling her into a hug. "Go get cleaned up and let me take over in here."

"I wanted to make you something special."

Your being here is special. In that moment, he realized how much he'd grown to care for both. But what was the point? Whatever they shared couldn't end happily. He was damaged goods—inside and out. "Go on. I've got this."

"But the kitchen is such a mess."

So is my head.

"Let me at least help clean."

"Nope…" He passed her the baby, then propelled them both toward the bathroom. "Take care of our little flour monster, then we're going to have a proper Christmas morning with bacon and eggs and presents."

She looked crestfallen. "I didn't get you anything."

"No worries. Santa brought plenty for everyone."

"But—" She'd spun to face him, no doubt to launch a fresh protest, but Gideon wasn't having it. Might be what little remained of the SEAL in him, but he liked establishing a plan, then following it. Which was why it made no sense for him to want nothing more than to kiss her quiet.

He slipped his hand under the fall of her wild nest of hair, drawing her close, fully planning to kiss her.

Her pupils dilated and lips slightly parted.

She leaned in.

He leaned in.

Chip squirmed and cried.

As if forcing herself from a daze, Jane shook her head, then nodded toward the bathroom. "I, ah, guess I'll get cleaned up. Thanks for your sweet offer to clean and cook."

"No problem." What was a problem? His craving to take whatever they shared much further than friendship.

In no time, he'd cleaned the kitchen and had bacon sizzling in a cast-iron skillet. He followed the directions on a box of blueberry muffin mix Mrs. Gentry must have left in the pantry, then put them in the oven.

While they baked, he stoked the fire, turned on the Christmas tree lights, assembled the gifts and tried pretending that the whole time he hadn't been imaging Jane standing naked in his shower.

When they emerged, he'd set the table and breakfast was ready.

"This looks and smells amazing," she said, unwittingly swelling his chest with pride. "Thank you."

"You're welcome. Now, let's eat so we can get to presents."

Her laugh made Gideon's spirit soar. If only they could freeze time, making a forever loop of this day. But they couldn't, which made him all the more determined to make what would undoubtedly be their last holiday together all the more special.

With breakfast done, Gideon ushered Jane toward the sofa. She held Chip on her lap.

"Santa brought each of you three gifts. Want to open your big ones first, or little?"

Grinning, she consulted her son. "What do you think?"

He burped.

"I think I heard big?" Gideon teased.

"Me, too." Her smile was his best gift ever.

Gideon passed her one box, then another much larger. "You might as well open these together."

"Okay…" His wrapping with green foil paper was crude. But it was the thought that counted, right? "Oh, Gideon… It's adorable!" She plopped the pint-sized black felt cowboy hat on Chip's little head. It was still too large, but he'd grow into it. The bittersweet question was, would Gideon be around to see it? Jane had opened her gift, drawing out a black wool cowboy hat with pink embroidery on the hat band and underside of the brim. After putting it on, she said, "I love it! Thank you!"

"You're welcome. Open this one next."

"But as soon as I get Chip and me unburied, I was going to give you a hug."

"Don't worry about it. We'll hug it out when you're done."

"Sounds like a plan."

Damn, she made a cute cowgirl.

He handed her another box. "This one is for Chip. He might be a little young, but I want you thinking long-term."

She laughed. "Duly noted." After unwrapping a state-of-the-art drone, she said with a grin, "Fess up, mister. Did you buy this for yourself?"

"Maybe. But I do think Chip needs to bone up on his aviation skills."

"Right. We'll get on that—just as soon as he figures out how to find his feet."

"Deal. Open this one." Gideon was having so much fun, he wished he'd bought more gifts just to watch her open them.

"You're awful…" Her words might have been salty, but her smile was huge. In the box was nestled a long-sleeved bigfoot T-shirt. It read I Saw Bigfoot and Sasquatched My Pants. "Seriously, you're so mean. It could have been a bigfoot growling that night in the woods."

"Did I say it wasn't?" He joined in her laughter.

She wadded a ball of wrapping paper and pitched it at him.

"Unwrap Chip's…"

Her baby was soon gumming a stuffed bigfoot.

"It's adorable. Thank you. For everything."

"You've got one more."

"Gideon…" She adjusted Chip's hat. "You've already done too much."

Impossible. He handed her the last gift. It was a small box. The kind that could be misconstrued for a ring.

"It's not a big deal. I just thought they would look pretty against your hair."

By the time he finished rambling, she'd opened the red velvet box that held gold and freshwater pearl earrings.

"These are stunning. You shouldn't have…"

"I got a good deal."

"Regardless… Really, thank you so much. For everything. I'm not sure how I know, but I feel like this is my best Christmas ever."

"For a woman with no memory, I suppose it would be."

She stood, nestling Chip among the wrappings. Grinning, she asked, "How about that hug?"

I thought you'd never ask…

"SORRY I WASN'T here sooner." Later that morning, Mrs. Gentry bustled through the cabin's door, arms laden with stacked casserole dishes. "The dogs got out, and then Peter Ivanov popped in for coffee."

"Who's that?" Jane took the dishes from her friend, nudging the door closed behind her with her foot.

"He and his cousin, Igor, live in the trailer down the road a piece from mine. They're good enough boys. A little strange, but then aren't we all for living out on this lonely mountain? Hope you don't mind, but I invited them for supper."

"That's fine, but will we have enough chairs?"

"They can sit on hay bales."

Jane laughed. And it felt good. Gideon was outside, working with Jelly Bean. As much as she usually enjoyed his company, after their Christmas morning, which felt like an intimate family occasion, she was glad for the breathing room. "Mind if I ask you a question?"

"Shoot. But be quick about it. We've got about fifteen grocery bags to carry in."

"Do you think Gideon's lost his mind for wanting to back me in the bakery?"

She snorted. "His mind's all right. His heart? That's another matter."

Jane's heart fluttered. "What do you mean?"

She made sure Chip was secure in his infant seat before chasing after Mrs. Gentry out the door.

"He told me he doesn't like me—in a romantic way."

"Are you two in grammar school? No man in his right mind would try renting a woman a bakery unless he has the hots for her. Plain and simple, the man's over the moon about you and your baby boy. He just doesn't know how to show it—aside from backing you in a business. Which I must say is a tad unconventional, but a man once wooed me by rototilling my garden."

"What happened?" Jane took three reusable canvas totes from the trunk of Mrs. Gentry's Oldsmobile.

"What do you think? I married him. Mr. Gentry and I shared forty years before he went and got himself killed by cancer. There's not a day goes by that I don't miss him. But you mark my words, Gideon might not admit what he's feeling for you, but his actions speak loud and clear. Be patient. He'll come around."

Jane prayed her friend was right.

Since she'd baked the desserts either early that morning or the night before, Jane turned the kitchen over to Mrs. Gentry while she focused on decorating the barn.

Earlier in the week, in between baking cookies and taking Chip to another well-child visit with Dr. Childress, Jane also had her last postdelivery visit. She'd summoned her courage to ask when she could have sex. The doctor told her that theoretically, whenever her body told her she was ready, she wouldn't be hurt. But most doctors agreed six weeks was the norm. She was disappointed, but shouldn't have been. It wasn't as if Gideon was giving her much *action*.

For days, she'd been making pine boughs, and now used a ladder to hang them from the lower rafters.

It took two red tablecloths to cover the plank table Gideon had assembled, then she ran more pine sprigs down the center, interspersing them with white candles and holly trimmings from the bush she'd found in Gideon's side yard.

"Think you might have any use for this?" Gideon stepped up behind her carrying clusters of mistletoe.

"Thanks. I'll hang it from the rafters. Mrs. Gentry sounds as if she may be sweet on this man named Peter, and in need of kissing. Do you know him? Is he good enough for her?"

"Don't you worry. The woman sleeps with a rifle at the head of her bed. It's him you should pray for."

Jane laughed. One of these days—preferably sooner than later—he'd realize how much he needed to kiss her, and that would be that. The three of them would live happily ever after.

Jane climbed back up the ladder with the mistletoe, hanging it with the same florist wire she'd used on the pine boughs. With Gideon holding the ladder steady, her body grew hyperaware. Of course, she wanted her own kiss beneath the mistletoe, but she was done putting moves on him. The next one was all on Gideon.

Finished, she headed down, not a bit disappointed when he grasped her waist, ensuring she made it safely onto the plank floor.

"I have to admit—" he gazed over his head "—you did a nice job. The barn looks great."

"Thank you for the table. Where did you get the benches?"

"Made them. Didn't take long."

"That was seriously sweet."

"Yeah, well, don't go spreading it around town that I have a soft spot for a cute brunette and her baby boy."

"Mum's the word." She adored Gideon when he was in one of his flirty moods. All she wanted for Christmas was for him to stay like this the entire day, forgetting the reasons he supposedly had for why they wouldn't work, replacing them with reasons why they could.

"THIS LOOKS LIKE a photo straight from Pinterest," Sherrie said when she stepped into the barn. "Everything is perfect." She gave Jane a bottle of wine and a big hug.

Gideon watched the proceedings from in front of Jelly Bean's stall. He held the baby, and was surprised to find himself feeling proud of not only Jane, but himself for helping to put this party together. He'd rigged up his satellite radio so they had a steady stream of carols from all eras and artists.

Mrs. Gentry held court beside the table, flirting up a storm with Igor and his brother. She'd invited six additional neighbor families he'd never met—three little girls and two boys chased one another with happy squeals.

"This is some shindig." West approached, drinking from a longneck beer.

"I'm surprised you came."

"Wouldn't have if I hadn't detected a note of desperation in your re-invitation."

Gideon finished his own beer. "See Jane? How happy she is. That's why you're here. I'd just as soon spit on you as look at you."

"Duly noted," West said. "For what it's worth, I owe you an apology. When I told the mayor about you and me having words, she let me have it. It seems she thinks as highly of Jane as you."

"She's an amazing gal. I should charge you admission for the privilege of tasting her cooking."

West busted out laughing.

"I'm not kidding," Gideon said with a growl.

"I know. What else do you think would be so damned funny?"

The day meandered like a lazy river, ebbing and flowing with great food and conversation. As expected, Jane's desserts were the stars of this show.

The looser the crowd got on beer and Mrs. Gentry's champagne punch, the taller tales grew and the more couples paired off to dance. Outside, wind from an approaching storm wailed, but inside, the barn was toasty. The dozens of candles Jane lit lent a soft, romantic glow.

Not that Gideon was typically into that sort of thing, but he found his chest swelling with pride for Jane's latest accomplishment. She never failed to surprise him in good ways. Buzzed from too many beers and frosted sugar cookies, the thought occurred to him that as kind and sweet and good as she was, she might be the one woman in a thousand who wouldn't think less of him because of his leg.

But how did a man broach such a thing? *Oh, hey, I failed to mention it when we first met, but I've only got one leg.*

"Care to dance, cowboy?" For the first time in hours, Gideon found himself alone with Jane. He was just drunk enough to forget his reality.

He nodded, then eased his arm around Jane's waist, drawing her close. He no longer carried the weight of his dead ex or his leg that had been blown to hell. He was just a man. It was Christmas, and Jane was a desirable woman with whom he cared to share a slow country song.

She wore a silky red dress that made it all too easy for him to skim his hands up her back, pressing her tightly enough for her breasts to mound against him. His erection throbbed, told him all manner of things he wanted to do instead of dancing, but because she was his Jane, he settled for this sweet slice of dance-floor heaven.

"Thank you for helping with the party." She tipped her head back, staring up at him with her sleepy-sexy gaze that secretly always drove him wild. "I think this should become an annual thing."

Me, too. But for that to happen, he'd need to man up and tell her about his leg. But that was okay. This was sweet Jane. She wouldn't hurt him. She would never turn her back on him like his ex.

"You blew me away with this whole night, Jane. Of course you should do it again." All he'd have to do to kiss her full, pouty lips would be bow his head forward a fraction of an inch. It would be so simple, yet could potentially prove his unraveling.

"Thank you, Gideon. Coming from you, that means a lot." Her pupils dilated, and she held her lips slightly apart. Her warm breath fanned his mouth, making him want her more.

"Look who's under the mistletoe!" Mrs. Gentry danced by, holding two red Solo cups filled with champagne punch. "Kiss her, you big fool."

The couples around them laughed.

No one at the party besides Mrs. Gentry, Sherrie and West knew about Gideon's disability. Truth was, probably no one cared. He was almost certain his angelic Jane wouldn't. But what happened when she saw him in the bedroom? He would die if the look on her face brought to light his every worst fear—that she saw him as only half a man.

Palms sweating, heart racing, he wanted to tell her his whole truth, but not as badly as he craved moving the half inch forward to brush his lips against hers.

Three...

Two...

One...

Sweet Lord, they had contact. Judging by her sexy gasp, soon followed by a groan when he slipped her his tongue, she'd been waiting for this as long as he had. Everything about the two of them just fit. He couldn't describe it. Didn't understand it. All he knew was that if he didn't want to lose her, he'd better wise up quick.

He needed to once and for all come to terms with the fact that his leg wasn't coming back, but with Jane and Chip in his life, there was a good chance his happiness could.

Gideon kissed her and kissed her until they were both out of breath and laughing before going for it all over again.

"The doctor said I have to wait six weeks until..." Her shy smile told him exactly what she meant. "But that doesn't mean I can't...you know...do you."

"No." She had no clue what she was saying. The visual image of her between his leg and stump physically made him ill.

Gideon ran for the barn doors and the moment he was outside, lost his meal in the weeds.

Of course, Jane followed, rubbing her hand comfortingly along his back. "Think you might have had too much to eat or drink?"

"Both," he said with a strangled laugh. What had he been thinking? He was no more ready to tell her about his leg than she was ready to hear. He'd use the fact that she literally couldn't have sex to his advantage. They'd take the time to practice kissing. Lots and lots of kissing.

"Can I get you anything?" she asked. "There's ginger ale someone brought for a cocktail mix."

"I'm good," he lied.

She stood shivering in a pool of the barn's light. Wind and snow whipped her hair, making her look like a supermodel on an arctic shoot.

"Let's get you warm." He led her back into the barn. On the outside, he held up his party guy demeanor.

On the inside? Even days later, the mental image of Jane up close and personal with his stump refused to leave his head.

"I SHOULD PINCH MYSELF," Jane said to Gideon New Year's Eve upon entering the inn's glittering ballroom. She'd pumped enough milk for Mrs. Gentry to watch Chip, and Gideon had booked them the same room she'd loved her last stay. Only this time, they were sharing it. Her heart didn't dare think too much about the implications of what that might mean, but her needy body did. Too bad she hadn't received the okay from Dr. Childress. But he did say her body was ultimately the judge. Was four weeks good enough? A frustrating hum between her legs said it was. "This is going to be the best night ever."

"Agreed." Gideon took her hand, leading her straight to the crowded dance floor. Prince's "1999" played, but

Gideon held her as if it were a slow song, using the opportunity to nuzzle her neck, then blaze a trail of kisses up her throat and jaw and finally, perfectly land them on her lips.

The change in him since Christmas had been remarkable.

She couldn't put her finger on it, but something about him had fundamentally changed. It was as if he'd been at war with himself about a personal issue that no longer held importance. Considering her own demons, who was she to judge his?

She needed to tell him the truth about her past. But the timing had never seemed right. Especially when it changed nothing.

Back in Phoenix sat a big, empty house that her accountant had long ago been instructed to handle. Before leaving on her hike, she'd told her entire legal team that she didn't know when she'd be back. Her ob-gyn had been mortified, imploring her not to go, but she didn't know the emotional pain and embarrassment Allison had gone through. Deacon not only stole her heart, but the business that had been her soul. Sugar Rush hadn't been merely a career for her, but her family.

Now she had a new family. Friends.

On a break between kisses, she said, "You're taller than me and able to see over the masses. Are Sherrie and West here yet?"

"I haven't seen them, but can't say I've been looking. Ever since I first saw you in that gold number, I haven't been able to take my eyes off you. You look hot."

"Thank you." His praise warmed her like summer sun. She'd borrowed the strapless sequined cocktail dress from Sherrie. It was snug in the bosom, but

Gideon didn't seem to mind. "You're looking awfully cute yourself—even with your hat head."

"Hey—I brushed it like you said. It's just stuck that way."

"I'm not complaining." She stroked his hair back, beyond pleased that wherever they stood in their undefined relationship, she was now allowed to touch him as much as she liked.

"Before we meet up with Sherrie and West, I want to run something by you."

"O-okay..." She searched his expression and found a muscle ticking in his set jaw. "Is everything all right?"

"Sure." He forced a deep breath. "I just need to get something clear with you, and with us being on the verge of welcoming a new year, I figure now is the perfect time."

"There are some quiet tables over there." She pointed to a shadowy area well beyond the dance floor.

The historic oval-shaped ballroom had been decked out in shimmering gold. Hundreds of gold balloons had risen to the ceiling; their spiraling metallic tails made a sparkly forest that kissed the tops of their heads. Dozens of round tables had been dressed in white and gold linens. Towering topiary centerpieces had been made of white roses and gold balls. Even though it was snowing outside—as it had been for days—the space smelled like a spring garden. Lights were dim, and candles shimmered on each glitter-sprinkled table.

Jane had been enchanted, but on the walk to the table, her stomach knotted. What if Gideon was on the verge of confessing whatever secret he'd been hiding, then proposing? Or what if he confessed, then told her this was the last time he wanted to be with her?

All air had been sucked from her lungs. The once-happy butterflies in her belly rioted.

Having reached the table, he pulled out a chair for her.

She sat.

He angled his chair to face her, then joined her, taking her hands for a squeeze. That couldn't be a bad sign, right?

"You look scared," he said. "Please don't. It's my hope that what I'm about to tell you changes nothing. If it does—" he grinned, stroking the tops of her hands with his thumbs "—we're golden. If it doesn't? Well…" He dropped his gaze. "Guess we were never meant to be."

"Out with it already. What could you possibly be hiding that I don't already know?"

The DJ played Justin Timberlake's "Can't Stop the Feeling," and it seemed as if everyone present was having the time of their lives except for the two of them.

"I want to tell you," Gideon said, "but don't know how. I don't want you to—"

The music abruptly stopped.

The overhead lights were switched on.

The woman Jane recognized as the inn's manager stepped onto the DJ's temporary stage and took his mic. "I'm sorry to interrupt the party, but there's been an avalanche on Mountain Vista Road. Many cars have been buried, and the sheriff's department has asked for all able-bodied men to help look for survivors."

Jane covered her mouth with her hands.

Gideon stood. "I'm sorry, but I have to help."

"Absolutely. I'll see if here's anything I can do."

"One last thing," the manager said into the mic. "The mayor is missing and feared one of the victims." Her voice caught, and she wiped away tears. "W-we all love Sherrie, and if you would, please say a prayer for her and her baby to be found alive."

Why was this happening? Jane adored her new friend. Sherrie and West made the sweetest couple.

Gideon framed her face with his hands, kissing her with added intensity. "We'll find her. I..." He seemed as if he wanted—needed to say more, but then closed his mouth. "Sorry your big night was ruined. I'll make it up to you, okay?"

She nodded, but it didn't matter.

Nothing mattered but making sure their friend was safe.

THE AVALANCHE SCENE was sheer chaos.

Cars had been knocked off the road and stood on end, headlights beaming toward the still-snowing black sky. Some vehicles had been forced upside down, so that the taillights were all that showed. With New Year's Eve parties planned at every B and B, hotel and restaurant in town, traffic had been bumper-to-bumper. Who knew how many more cars were completely buried, serving as potential coffins for the occupants inside.

"Listen up!" West shouted through a loudspeaker to the hundred or so men gathered. "We've got shovels and picks piled alongside the ambulance. Let's do this as systematically as possible so no survivors are missed. Nathan and Paul brought their dozers, so let's let them do the heavy lifting, then we'll get in to help people out. I'll lead one team with Nathan and Deputy Hall will lead the other team with Paul. My goal is to have our friends and family safely out of here before the clock hits midnight. Got it?"

All assembled cheered in agreement.

Then got to work.

On and on they worked into the night. Families and couples were saved. Some without a scratch; others with broken bones and bruising were taken to the hospital.

Many women came to help—Jane was among them—to serve sandwiches and steaming coffee. The inn had a catering truck, so they'd set it up as a base of support crew operations.

"Any sign of Sherrie?" Jane asked at 1:00 a.m., handing Gideon a steaming cup of black coffee.

"Not yet."

"How is West holding up?"

"Not good. I guess Sherrie was on her way to the inn, but drove separate from him, because he had to answer a domestic disturbance call. She hasn't answered her cell. We've had one fatality—a female tourist up from Phoenix for the holiday. Her husband's in ICU. West lost it when he heard the news. I don't know what he'll do if he loses Sherrie and the baby. Hell—the whole town will fall apart. Everyone loves her."

"Then we'll just have to believe she's okay."

By 3:00 a.m., nine cars had been unearthed from the snow. One—a Mercedes—had no occupants. The windows were broken, but the tempered glass held them in place, meaning if there had been a driver and passengers inside, they hadn't been thrown out.

There was still no sign of the mayor.

Chapter Seventeen

By dawn, Jane counted that fourteen cars had been removed from the scene, five more people had died, and there was only twenty feet of snow to remove before reaching the undisturbed highway on the avalanche's other side.

Snow had stopped falling, but a bitter cold had set in.

Wind lashed volunteers' exposed cheeks and noses. Jane had made a run to Kingman's to buy all their ski masks and coffee.

"Sheriff!" a man called over the wind. "We found her car!"

Sherrie drove a cherry-red ragtop Jeep that allowed her to reach all her citizens in any weather.

Volunteers who'd stayed through the night ran in that direction. Both dozers worked to clear a path for the shovel brigade.

Jane watched in horror as the Jeep was unearthed, only to show the roof had caved in, crushing Sherrie and her unborn child beneath the weight of the snow. The rescue mission had instantly changed to body recovery.

West fell to his knees on the ground, wailing as if he were a wounded animal. Gideon went to him, kneeling beside him.

Silent tears streaming down her cheeks, Jane wasn't sure whether to intrude upon this most private moment.

As news of Sherrie's death spread through the volunteer camp, more cries rose above the wind. This situation was beyond awful. Unfathomable. It made Jane realize how perilously short life was, and how lucky she was to still have Gideon and her son.

West's family lived in Denver and Sherrie's in LA.

One of the deputies said he would place the necessary calls.

Gideon led West to his truck.

Once the sheriff was safely in the passenger seat, Gideon jogged to Jane. "I'm going to run him home. Want to ride along or stay?"

"You go. I'll help the other women clean up and feed the last few volunteers."

Mouth pressed tight, he nodded, then pulled her into a heartbreakingly strong hug. "Later, we need to talk. But only about good things, okay?" He drew back to meet her gaze, and the expression on his face held deep affection. "Sherrie's death, as tragic as it is, gave me a well-needed smack against the side of my head. Life's short. I never want to spend another day without you and Chip in it."

"Yes," she said through fresh tears. Her heart sang. She would tell him everything she'd learned about her past later, but for now, in the heart of this crisis, all that mattered was that they had each other.

THE RIDE TO West's home was somber.

He and Sherrie lived in an A-frame above town that had a sweeping valley view. The only way to reach it was by passing the crumpled remains of Sherrie's car. The county coroner had already taken her body.

"I need to make arrangements," West said.

"You don't need to do shit." Gideon slipped his truck into four-wheel drive to tackle the steep, unplowed road.

"Do you think she suffered?"

"No." Gideon's heart hurt for his friend. "My best guess? It was over before she'd even realized what hit her."

West nodded. "I don't know how to live without her. And the baby... God, our baby boy. My *son*."

"It's not easy." *But since meeting Jane, I know it's possible to live again.* It was way too soon to tell West that, but Gideon saw this as a wake-up call. Fate had delivered him the ultimate second chance and no way was he going to screw it up. If Jane learned about his handicap and couldn't handle it, that was on her. As soon as he got West settled, Gideon planned on finding Jane, then, if she'd have him, taking her to that wedding chapel on the outskirts of town.

West's home was far more grand than Gideon's cabin. He and Sherrie socialized a lot, and the couple had always planned on having three or four kids.

West's posture upon entering was one of total loss and devastation. He collapsed onto a leather sofa, dropped his head back and closed his eyes.

Gideon closed the door and walked straight to the wet bar, pouring a couple fingers of whiskey for them both.

"Here." He handed the tumbler to his friend. "It'll take the edge off."

West took it, knocking the whole thing back.

On the side table was an infant's crib mobile—tiny cop cars. It was still in the box, waiting to be assembled. West picked up the box, only to hurl it across the room.

Gideon sat on the love seat opposite his friend. Aside

from the view, a towering stone fireplace served as the focal point of the room. Three stockings had been hung. *Mommy, Daddy* and *West Jr.* Hung above the mantel was a wedding portrait of West in a tux and Sherrie in her heavily beaded, long-trained gown. She had been radiant. So happy. Gideon had spent most of their special day in a beer fog, feeling sorry for himself.

All of that seemed like another life.

Now, with Jane and her son, Gideon's future had never looked brighter. It made him feel bad about finally being happy. As if he were a traitor to his friend.

"Got any more of this?" West wagged his glass.

Gideon gave him a refill.

And then the two men just sat, the weight of the quiet house nearly as crushing as that of the killer snow.

JANE RODE WITH Amelia back to the inn.

While waiting for Gideon, she called Mrs. Gentry to check on Chip, pumped her aching breasts, then took a long soak in the room's claw-foot tub.

Mrs. Gentry had heard about the avalanche and Sherrie and assured Jane that Chip was getting along fine.

Eyes closed, Jane visualized how different her New Year's Eve was supposed to have been. What secret had Gideon been on the verge of spilling? Considering recent events, did it even matter?

Life was moving too fast.

She needed it to slow down. But at the same time, when it came to her relationship with Gideon, the sooner they cemented their bond with permanent vows, the better.

She dressed in a comfy jogging suit, ate a chocolate-covered strawberry from the celebratory champagne tray she'd ordered for what was supposed to have been their late-night snack, and then curled onto the settee, watching a classic Goldie Hawn movie, but never paying full attention since she was constantly looking toward the door.

Nearing lunchtime, there was finally a knock.

Jane muted the TV and raced to answer, but instead of Gideon as she'd expected, a uniformed police officer greeted her, hat in hand. "Hello, ma'am. I'm Deputy Paul Walletta from the Pine Glade Sheriff's Office."

"Yes. I recognize you from the rescue efforts." She clutched the throat of her zip-front jacket, willing her pulse to slow. "Is this about Gideon? Is he all right?"

"Gideon Snow? I'm not sure. I mean, I suppose he's fine—as far as I know, he's still with the sheriff. I'm here about another matter. May I come in?"

Gaze narrowed, beyond uncomfortable, Jane welcomed the man inside, leading him to the room's table. "Please, have a seat."

He did, then set a clear plastic Baggie in front of him. Inside rested a pink Chanel wallet and keys.

"Would you like anything to eat or drink?"

"No, ma'am. But thank you. Ordinarily, this sort of thing would be handled by the sheriff, but since—well, I'm sure you'll understand that he's probably not feeling up to a matter such as this."

"Of course." Her heart beat faster by the second. What was this about?

He opened the Baggie, eased out the wallet, then presented it to her. "First, I guess I should ask if you're the woman folks around here have been referring to as Jane Doe?"

"I am…" Mouth dry, Jane realized this was the moment her worlds collided.

"An odd thing happened during that avalanche. It

originated at a point high above one of the forest service's lookout points. It took out the entire bluff-side
parking area. A team of government fellas went up there
this morning by snowmobile to check the area's over-
all stability—it's not good." The man tugged at his collar. "It is warm in here. Do you have a bottled water?"

She took one from the minibar, handing it to him.

"Thank you, ma'am. If you were at the avalanche
scene, you may have recalled that one of the cars we
recovered was a silver Mercedes. The license number
is—"

Another knock sounded on the door. This time, Jane
prayed it wasn't Gideon. She knew she'd have to eventually tell him about her past, but not now. Not like this.

Jane froze.

"Don't you need to get that?"

She gulped. Shook her head.

The knocking persisted. "Jane! It's Gideon. Let me
in!"

"Ma'am?" The deputy cocked his head, narrowed
his gaze. "Is everything okay?"

"Fine." Dizzy, hot, nauseous, Jane somehow stumbled her way from the table to the door. She opened it
to be pulled into a bear hug.

"It's about time," Gideon said. "What took you so
long? West is a mess, and I feel horrible, but right now, I
think you and I need to get a few things out of the way."

"Gideon—" He put his fingers over her lips.

"Let me go first. I've been a fool. There's something
I should have told you the first day we met, but I was
too big of a coward. Now I realize that and—"

The deputy cleared his throat. His cheeks turned the
same shade as the strawberries. "Mr. Snow." He tipped
his hat. "How is the sheriff?"

"About as good as could be expected. What's this about?" He looked from the deputy to Jane. "I don't mean to be rude, but Paul, why are you here?"

They gravitated to the table, where the deputy began anew for Gideon's benefit.

There was a Shamrock Inn postcard on the table. Jane used it to fan her overheated face.

"What I guess I'm trying to say," the deputy rambled while Gideon listened with rapt interest, "is that Jane Doe, we believe we know who you are. Everyone down at the sheriff's office is convinced that Mercedes parked up at the lookout must have been yours. If it weren't for the avalanche, no one would have found it till spring thaw. Go ahead and look through your wallet. It was found wedged under the driver's seat. Your appearance matches your license. Your name is Allison Ford, and you're kind of a big deal. We made a few preliminary calls to emergency contacts in Phoenix and they confirmed that you've been missing. Your lawyer should be on his way later this afternoon to pick you up."

"No. Call him back. I don't want to go." Head bowed, gaze focused on her wringing hands, she whispered, "If I'd wanted to see him, I already would have."

"What do you mean?" Gideon asked. "How could you have called if— Wait." The color drained from his face. "You knew. Your memory came back and you knew. All those spells at the cabin? The headaches? How long, Jane? How long have you known?"

"N-not long." Silent tears streamed down her cheeks. She left the table in search of a tissue.

Unfortunately, Gideon followed.

"Anyway!" the deputy called. "I'll be going. Ms. Ford, I wanted to drop off your wallet and let you know our office will be happy to help in any way we can."

Once the deputy was gone, Jane said to Gideon, "I'm sorry. I love you. I didn't think my past mattered."

"You love me?" Gideon laughed. "You sure have a funny way of showing it. I was on my way over here to ask you to marry me. I was going to tell you that life is too short to waste a second, and that we need to seal this crazy deal the two of us have going. But what's the point? You have a whole other life you've been keeping from me for weeks."

"What are you talking about? From the very beginning, from the first time I saw you, I knew you were the one. I've been through so much, Gideon. Chip's father ripped my company out from under me. Then he tossed us both aside as if we were trash. He was in it for the thrill of the game. Ruining our lives was sport. What I shared with you was real. How could it be anything else? You have to believe me."

"I do." Head bowed, he said, "I'm sorry. All these weeks, your former life has been ticking between us like a time bomb. But now that we've both found out, it's no doubt time for you to go. I have total faith in you to do amazing things with your life. Staying here would only tie you down. You deserve to fly."

"Every time I'm with you, that's how you make me feel." She stood on her tiptoes to kiss him. Their lips collided, sparking like lightning trapped in a bottle.

She ripped at his shirt.

He jerked down her jacket's zipper.

Their kisses were frantic and sloppy. He dragged down her pants, and she fumbled with his fly. He lifted her onto the bathroom counter, kissing her neck and chest. She cried out.

She clawed at him, drawing him closer. Doctor's

orders be damned. She needed Gideon inside her now. *Forever.*

"I love you," she cried out when he lifted her, spreading her legs to plunge inside. There was a moment's pain, but then steadily rising, spiraling, dizzying pleasure. Higher and higher they climbed until reaching the zenith of everything they were and would ever be.

Finally, this was the physical manifestation of their love.

Jane couldn't stop crying.

"Did I hurt you?"

She shook her head. "I-I wanted to tell you who I was, but I was afraid you would make me leave. I was in the woods that day to hide from everyone I've ever known. I told my attorney and friends I'd be on a local Phoenix trail, but at the last minute changed my mind. I know better than to hike without sharing my plan— especially this time of year. I put myself and my baby at risk and it was stupid. Reckless. I could have died. Maybe a part of me selfishly wanted to die? How's that for a shameful confession?"

For too long Gideon stayed silent. Being with Jane in a physical way had been more than he ever could have wanted. But while she'd come clean, he still hadn't. The mere prospect of telling her about his leg, only to have her reject him like Missy had, made his heart hammer. "Paul said you're a big deal. What did he mean?"

"Ever heard of Sugar Rush?"

"The cookie chain?" His eyebrows raised. "It was my last stop before going on missions and my first stop when coming home. Everyone on the planet has heard of Sugar Rush—it's akin to McDonald's. That's yours?"

"Not anymore." She laughed through more tears. "I lost it—that was my first act of sheer stupidity."

"But you're still rich, right? Used to the finer things in life?" *Everything and everyone being perfect? Especially any guy in your life?* No way would she *ever* want to be with a one-legged man. He withdrew from her, breaking their sexual and emotional connection.

"No. I'm not like that at all. You know me, Gideon. I'm Jane. Content living in your cabin. All I want is a simple life with you and our son. I want you to adopt Chip. The three of us will be so happy."

He sharply exhaled. Adjusted himself back into his boxers, then pulled up his pants and zipped his fly. "I've got to go."

"What do you mean? Stay. We'll shower. Get something to eat. Then go pick up Chip together."

He shook his head. "This—me and you. It isn't working. I told you from the start it never would."

"What are you talking about?" Tears streamed down her cheeks. "We made love. It was beautiful."

"It was sex. Nothing more." He was lucky God didn't strike him dead for lying. What they'd shared had been perfect. He loved her so much it hurt. He loved her so much that he didn't want her feeling trapped upon hearing his news.

"Bastard!" She threw the plastic tissue holder at him, but missed. It shattered against the wall and clattered to the tile floor. "Go! I don't love you! I never want to see you again!"

Her words cut like glass.

She cried so hard, he doubted she'd even seen him leave. Would her soul ache as much as his when he was gone?

Chapter Eighteen

"Oh my…" Mrs. Gentry passed Jane the baby. "After hearing that news, I need to sit down."

Upon realizing she had a wallet filled with credit cards bearing her name, not only had Jane paid the inn's bill in full, but she'd bought an SUV with four-wheel drive.

From the car lot, she'd driven to Kingman's to pick up an infant car seat and basic supplies. It wouldn't be a long trip to Phoenix. She remembered having set up a nursery in her home there. As for Chip's things at Gideon's cabin? As far as she was concerned, they could stay there. She and Gideon were done.

"You're the closest thing to a movie star I've ever met. I feel like asking for your autograph."

"That's silly. I'm just Jane."

"But your name is Allison Ford. You own one of the biggest cookie companies in the world."

"*Used* to own it. Now stockholders and a big fat board of directors are in charge. I'm not even allowed in the corporate headquarters."

"I'm so sorry," her friend said. "At least you still have Gideon. Where is he, by the way? Why isn't he with you?"

Jane gave her the G-rated version of his abrupt exit.

"So just like that, you're leaving?"

"I was hoping you'd do me a favor." Jane opened her wallet and wrote a check. Handing it to her friend, she asked, "After I'm gone, would you please run this to Gideon's cabin? If he's not there, leave it on the counter. It should be more than enough to cover what he spent feeding and housing Chip and me."

Mrs. Gentry took the check. Her eyes widened. "Jane—I mean, Allison—this is for fifty thousand dollars. Gideon couldn't have spent anywhere near that amount on you."

"It's okay. There's plenty more where that came from. The last thing I want is to feel beholden to him or anyone else. From here on out, Chip and I are on our own."

"You'll always have me." The two women shared a hug, with Mrs. Gentry promising to visit soon.

Jane fastened Chip into his new safety seat, then climbed behind the wheel of her new car, ready to face her old life.

AFTER SHERRIE'S FUNERAL, Gideon's life hit a new low.

If it weren't for his promise to rehabilitate a dead girl's horse, he might never have left his bed.

He'd shredded Jane's ridiculous check.

Every inch of his cabin reminded him of Jane and her son. The Christmas tree still stood in the window, more needles dropping every day, but he couldn't bear taking it down.

She'd left everything. Her rainbow of jogging suits. Chip's toys, clothes and baby gear. Gideon knew he should box it up and donate it to someone who could use it, but to do that would somehow hurt worse than looking at it. It would essentially be erasing the two of them. And that was something he couldn't yet do.

Winter turned to spring.

Jelly Bean passed her final exams, and he transported her back to her family. They reported that she was doing fine.

Every trip into town for chicken or donkey feed, Gideon was forced to see the brown construction paper over the windows in the shop that he and Jane would have shared. The outside had been painted, a decadent amount of Victorian-style wood detailing added, each layer a different pastel color. The place resembled a slice of multicolored layer cake.

Comfy-looking custom benches had been added to both sides of the shellacked hot-pink door.

He already hated the new owners for stealing his dream.

But if he was being honest, he had to admit he hadn't really lost Jane, but driven her away, just as he had Missy.

How many times had he replayed their last moments together?

How many times had he regretted his reactionary behavior?

It was nearing Easter when he noticed a sign being installed on the shop front that was supposed to have been his and Jane's. The sight got him so flustered that he had to pull into a parking spot to watch. Giant hot-pink metal letters lined with white bulbs that would look sharp at night read Sweet Tooth. The font was a feminine script.

What the hell? The new owners used Jane's name?

His head knew her real name was Allison, but his heart would always know her as Jane.

With the sign installed, the show was over. He bought the few supplies he'd driven to town for, then headed back to his cabin.

Along the way, he noticed West's sheriff's department SUV parked at the bar on the south side of town. He hadn't seen his friend since the funeral. Gideon figured the right thing to do would be to at least buy the man a beer. At the same time, what would it hurt to find out a little something about these city slickers who'd bought his rental contract right out from under him.

"Hey, stranger." West sat at the bar, filling out a report. "Long time, no see."

"Likewise. How long have you been back on the job?"

"Couple weeks. I stayed a while with my folks. Took time to get my head on straight."

"I understand."

"How are things with you and Allison?"

"Who? Oh—you mean Jane."

"Duh. You two aren't together?"

"No." Gideon sat on a stool at the bar and ordered a beer. "Damn near the second she found out she was Ms. Fancy Pants, she took off for greener pastures."

Eyebrows raised, West said, "Interesting. That's not the version I heard."

"Who have you been talking to?"

"Pretty much everyone in town save for you. You broke things off with her because of your leg, didn't you?"

"That's none of your damned business." Gideon downed his beer in a single gulp, tapping the bar for another.

"It is when I would give *anything*—including my

left leg—to have my wife and son back. You never told her, did you?"

"Why would I? She wasn't my Jane anymore, but an accomplished businesswoman. What would she want with a broken-ass ex-SEAL like me?"

"Damned if I know. But considering all of that, I find it interesting that she's back in town."

"What do you mean?" Gideon's gaze narrowed.

"She didn't just rent herself a building for her bakery, but bought it. She's spared no expense in making it brand-new—top to bottom. Amelia told me her improvements have doubled the property value. She's planning her grand opening for Easter. I got my invitation last week. It was fancy. A giant decorated Easter egg cookie. Wildest thing I've seen in a while." He fell silent, tapping the bar with his pen. "Sherrie would have eaten that up. She loved fancy shit like that. Guess it's a woman thing."

"Guess so."

West finished his report on that afternoon's barroom brawl, then left to tackle a non-injury car crash.

Gideon sobered enough to drive home, fed his animals, then drank himself to sleep with a bottle of scotch he'd found stashed in a kitchen cabinet.

Jane and her son were back in town.

What was he supposed to do with that information?

He snorted. If he were smart, he'd march right over, apologize for being an ass, once and for all tell her about his leg, then ask her to be his wife. But all of that took courage. This wasn't his Jane he'd be dealing with, but a stranger who was only going through with opening her bakery to make more money. He was a fool to think it might have anything to do with him.

EASTER SUNDAY WAS a big day for Pine Glade.

It marked the unofficial start of the summer tourist season with the opening of the high mountain passes and most of the big ranch-style resorts.

Allison stood behind the counter of her bakery, hands trembling not because she had any doubts about her new venture succeeding, but because she prayed Gideon might be one of her customers. She'd tried denying it, but she still loved him. If she hadn't, she never would have gone ahead with what was supposed to have been their shared dream.

There was another reason she needed to be close to him.

One that wouldn't come to fruition for another five months. Pregnant with his child, she was barely showing. Beneath her frilly hot-pink apron, her secret was safe. She would tell him, but not until he finally came clean with whatever secret he held that had presumably been explosive enough to break them apart.

"Excited?" Mrs. Gentry asked. She and Amelia's daughter, Holly, were helping with the opening. It was intended to be an invitation-only event, but since pretty much the whole town had been invited, she hoped for a huge turnout.

"Very. Do you think he'll come?"

"Gideon?" Mrs. Gentry shrugged. "If you ask me, you could do better. I have more respect for the man's donkey."

"Aw, he's not all that bad."

"How can you say that? Especially when he broke things off so abruptly with you?"

"I guess I love him. Love has a way of forgiving actions that logic no doubt dictates I shouldn't."

Holly stood at the window and reported, "People are

already lining up outside." They'd kept the windows covered with brown butcher paper to heighten the element of surprise.

Allison had flown in a renowned commercial property decorator to make the place as over the top as Willy Wonka's factory. She wasn't just selling cookies, but pies, custom cakes, and both homemade and vintage candies. Giant wrapped candies hung from the ceiling. The tables looked like pink cakes with wedges for chairs. The walls were white with giant pink metallic polka dots. The counter stools resembled old-time Bazooka wrappers.

"Should we open the doors?" Holly asked.

Allison took a deep breath and nodded.

She'd waited a long time for this, and she should have been thrilled. This enchanting place would bring joy to everyone who passed through. What it couldn't do was bridge the rift between her and Gideon. The only person who could do that was him. Too bad he was nowhere to be found.

For the past few years, Gideon had spent Easter with Mrs. Gentry. Since he'd parted ways with Jane, his neighbor had given him the cold shoulder. Clearly, she'd picked sides in the breakup, and he hadn't won.

He spent that warm, sunny morning cleaning the chicken coop and getting the barn ready for a new horse that he'd pick up in Denver the next week. He mowed the lawn, weedeating the edges, then painted trim that the winter temperature extremes had cracked and faded.

He'd long since removed the Christmas tree, tossing it into his favorite pond for the fish. The handmade ornaments had been carefully tissue-wrapped and boxed the way he had a vague memory of his paternal grandmother doing when he'd been a small boy. As for the rest of Jane and Chip's belongings? They hadn't been touched. He couldn't bear to move them.

Around five that afternoon, he'd done all available chores and even gotten a jump start on his vegetable garden when a familiar four-wheeler revved over his freshly mowed lawn and rammed right into his stair rail.

Mrs. Gentry glared at him through her helmet.

Upon killing her engine, she took it off and looked as if she might be intent on killing him next. "Gideon Snow, you are a damn fool."

True. He had no doubt this lecture had something to do with Jane, and in every regard, he'd be first to admit he'd botched what had been a very good thing.

"What is wrong with you? West told me you know good and well that today was Jane's big opening, and yet you couldn't be troubled to stop by and congratulate her?"

"Wasn't invited." He turned his back on her to enter his cabin.

She followed. "The poor gal should have been over-the-moon happy. Instead she looked like a lovesick puppy. Every time the bell over the door jingled she looked up, hoping it would be you. And what's up with this shrine to her and Chip? If you don't still carry a torch for the girl, why isn't all of her and her baby's stuff gone?"

"I've been busy. And what she doesn't know is that by staying away, I did her a favor. Jane might have accepted me as damaged goods. Allison? No way. She's too good for me."

"Wait a gosh-darned minute." She slammed the front door. "Are you telling me the real reason you two broke up is because of your leg? She doesn't know?"

"Why would she?"

"Because when a man and woman sleep together..." Her complexion grew flush. "You're not dense. How in the world did you two make a baby without taking your clothes off?"

"She's pregnant?" He whipped around to face her. "She's carrying my baby?"

"Yes—but keep it to yourself, because she doesn't know I know. What I do know is that you'd better get your behind over there and make amends so the poor thing doesn't have to give birth all by herself again."

Mind spinning, Gideon didn't know what to do or think. All he did know what that he needed to see Jane right away.

ALLISON SAID GOODBYE to Holly and her last guest—there had been no paying customers today.

As amazing as Sweet Tooth's grand opening had been, a knot still felt wedged at the back of her throat.

"Did you have fun, sweetie?" Chip grinned, bucking in her arms. He now crawled and laughed and smiled. He had his tantrums, but they were quickly squelched with food, sleep or cuddles. For a month after leaving Gideon, he'd been fussy. Allison could only guess that her son had missed the only father figure he'd known. "I'll take that as a yes. But now, it's time for your bath, because you have frosting on your nose and tummy." Through his green-striped baby jumper, she tickled his chubby belly, earning a round of giggles.

After turning off the lights and locking the front and back doors, Allison headed up the stairs toward her apartment. It was small, but cozy, with a bedroom for her, a nook for Chip and a combined kitchen and living room. The lone bathroom could be accessed by her bedroom or the main living areas—not that she had many guests.

There was a knock on the front door.

"Sorry!" she sang out from upstairs. "But we're closed."

Knock, knock, knock. Whoever it was persisted.

"Jane—Allison! Let me in!"

She froze. *Gideon?*

Her name sounded strange coming from his lips.

"Please! We need to talk."

You think?

Angered that he'd just now reached this conclusion, she raced down the stairs, unfastened the lock, tossed open the door, and then caught sight of him and choked back a sob. "What happened? Are you sick?"

"Long story short—I miss you. And you…" He'd lost at least twenty pounds. Dark circles made his eyes look sunken. He was still the most handsome man she'd ever seen, but a shadow of his former self. He tickled Chip's belly, but instead of giggling, the baby cried.

"Come in." Allison stepped back, allowing him to enter, then closing the door behind him. He removed his worn black leather hat and still sported a ring of hat head. Her fingertips itched to smooth it flat. But when he'd gone, she'd lost that privilege. Odds were, she'd never get it back.

He gazed at the renovated space. "This is amazing. West says you're the talk of the town."

"That's nice of him to say. My goal was to create a space Pine Glade could be proud of. I wish Sherrie would have been here to cut an opening-day ribbon."

"She would have gotten a kick out of that."

With early-evening sun slanting through the picture windows, lending the space a fairy-tale glow, the strained silence between them felt even more awkward and out of place.

"Why are you here?" she finally asked, unable to bear a moment's more tension.

He fingered the rim of his hat, cleared his throat, then blurted, "A while back—I don't even recall when—I told you I just wanted to be friends. Do you remember?"

"Kinda hard to forget." She shifted the baby from one hip to her other. "Then you kissed me. Made love to me. Delivered promises with your body that your mouth decided not to keep."

"Sorry. I lied. Truth is—I love you, Jane Doe. Allison Ford. Doesn't matter what your name is, I love you. Hell, maybe I always have."

Her anger dissolved like salt in warm water. But not entirely. Not enough to keep from asking, "Then why did you hurt me? Say those horrible things once you learned who I really am? Why couldn't you accept the fact that fundamentally, nothing changed? I'm still the woman you've always known."

"Pride, okay? I couldn't live with the fact that you're perfect and I'm not."

"What are you talking about? I'm far from perfect. Newsflash—what happened with my company is now studied in business classes as an example of what not to do. I was a fool. I trusted a man who decimated me and I let him, so believe me, I'm about as far from perfect as a person can get."

"I'm not talking about your actions as a person. I'm talking about your body."

"What?" She wrinkled her nose. "I don't understand."

The baby grew antsy, so she crossed the room, setting him in the corner playpen she'd had built in so he could spend his days in the shop with her. He crawled to his favorite corner, flopped on top of a fluffy bunny, then gummed a car-shaped teething ring.

"He's gotten so big. Developed a personality."

"Babies do that. If you hadn't been such an ass, you would have had a front-row seat to his every new trick."

"I'm sorry. I had a good reason."

"That's right. Let's get back to it. I have a perfect body, and you're just some hard-bodied former Navy SEAL who fills out a pair of Wranglers better than any man I've ever seen. But go ahead, tell me about how imperfect you are and how that was your reason for bolting out the door about two minutes after we made love."

"I said I was sorry. I'm glad you like my ass, but you're going to hate this…" He sat on the nearest chair. He looked hopelessly out of place. The man she used to consider her big, tough cowboy awkwardly perched on a fake slice of cake.

"Stop being a drama queen, Gideon. I once told you I loved you and I meant it. Nothing you could do would…"

He'd rolled up the left leg of his faded Wranglers, then tugged off one of the dusty black cowboy boots she'd never seen him without. What she saw next brought instant tears to her eyes, and then anger in her heart, and then more love than she could even begin to express.

"Let me guess. You thought I would take one look at this amazing piece of technology that allows you to do everything any other man would despite you obviously having been through the kind of trying ordeal I can't even imagine, and then you automatically assumed I was shallow enough to no longer want you?

To no longer find you desirable? If I didn't love you so much, I would smack you for thinking so little of me."

She went to him, kneeling before him, kissing the arch of his artificial foot, and ankle and calf and the stocking covering his stump.

Allison glanced up to find tears shimmering in his eyes. "I. Love. *You*. All of you. Why would you keep this from me?"

Unable to speak, he shook his head. "Stupid pride. I love you so much, I'm so in awe of every single thing about you, I couldn't bear the thought of you not feeling the same about me."

"Then you're an idiot." She kissed the rest of her way up his leg, then rose to settle herself on his lap, turning her attention to his oh-so-kissable lips.

"Seems like I've heard that before."

He returned her kiss with a thrilling sweep of his tongue.

"I love every inch of you from your eternal hat-headed hair to your crooked grin that I finally coaxed out of you to the way you always rocked Chip to sleep faster than I ever could. Now, just like I had to be first to kiss you, am I going to have to ask you to marry me, too?"

"I kissed you first."

"No. I'm pretty sure I kissed you."

"Regardless, let me state for the record that I am officially proposing." He tugged a ring from his jeans pocket, then slipped it onto her left-hand ring finger. "Allison Ford, formerly known as Jane Doe, will you do me the honor of being my best friend, lover and wife?"

Crying happy tears, she nodded.

"Will you also allow me to adopt Chip so that I can be a father to him as well as his little brother or sister?"

"Wait—" She pulled back. "You know I'm pregnant? How?"

After a few seconds of thinking, she smiled. "Mrs. Gentry?"

They laughed, kissed and looked forward to the rest of their shared lives.

Epilogue

It had been a while since Gideon had rehabilitated a horse. These days, he mostly just rode them every chance he got when Allison had a break in between opening new stores.

In the year since their daughter had been born, Allison had opened three more Sweet Tooth shops, and he couldn't be prouder. Her business model was much different from her first time in the corporate world. This time around, she only built in small towns that had big tourist trades. With each grand opening, he loved watching her confidence bloom. Sure, since she was the family's main breadwinner, some might say she wore the pants in the family, but he preferred thinking of himself as their son and daughter's COP—chief operating parent.

On this warm June day in Breckenridge, Colorado, he sat on one of the store's signature front porch benches. Chip and Dale—he'd fought her on their daughter's name—napped in their stroller.

When Allison finally emerged, leaving the rest of the grand-opening festivities to Mrs. Gentry and Holly to hostess, she sat alongside him, resting her head on his shoulder. "I'm pooped."

"I don't blame you." He smoothed her hair, kissing

the crown of her head. "You know, it would be all right if you took a break."

"I know, but…"

"You'll never stop building your empire until it's bigger than Sugar Rush."

She sat up. "Am I that transparent?"

"Babe…" He kissed her long and leisurely before delivering a lecture she probably didn't want to hear. "In my eyes, you already are a hero. Now that you're pregnant again, don't you think it's time to slow down?"

"Is that a challenge? Do you think I can't do it all? Because—"

"Shh…" He kissed her quiet. "I have zero doubt that you can and will accomplish anything you set your mind to. My only question is should you? We have more than enough money to send these two to college for their doctorates, and still have enough left over for all four—soon to be five—of us to travel the globe. What we don't have is enough time. I miss baking with you and making salt dough ornaments."

"But what about my business? I can't lose it. It's my family."

"No, sweetheart—*we're* your family. I love you. The kids love you. As long as I'm alive, you'll never be alone again."

"Promise?"

He kissed her long and hard, assuring her with his body what he couldn't convey with words. Her love had been the key to making him whole again. What kind of husband would he be if he couldn't return the favor?

* * * * *

If you loved this book, look for more in
Laura Marie Altom's COWBOY SEALS *series:*

THE SEAL'S MIRACLE BABY
THE BABY AND THE COWBOY SEAL
THE SEAL'S SECOND CHANCE BABY
THE COWBOY SEAL'S JINGLE BELL BABY

Available now at Harlequin.com!

#1629 THE TEXAS VALENTINE TWINS

Texas Legacies: The Lockharts
by Cathy Gillen Thacker

Estranged lovers Wyatt Lockhart and Adelaide Smyth have a one-night stand resulting in twin babies. While figuring out how to coparent they discover they are already married!

#1630 HER COWBOY LAWMAN

Cowboys in Uniform • by Pamela Britton

Sheriff Brennan Connelly, champion former bull rider, reluctantly agrees to help Lauren Danners's son learn to ride bulls. But his attraction to the much younger single mom is a distraction he doesn't need!

#1631 THE COWBOY'S VALENTINE BRIDE

Hope, Montana • by Patricia Johns

An IED sent Brody Mason home from Afghanistan, but he's determined to go back. There's nothing for him in Hope, Montana...except maybe Kaitlyn Harpe, the nurse who's helping him to walk again, ride again and maybe even love again.

#1632 A COWBOY IN HER ARMS

by Mary Leo

Callie Grant is stunned—the daughter of her ex and former best friend is in her kindergarten class! Widower Joel Darwood thinks what might be best for him and his child is Callie, if only he can convince her she's changed...

Get 2 Free Books,

♦HARLEQUIN® Western Romance

Plus 2 Free Gifts—
just for trying the Reader Service!

"I never knew you had a bit of a lawyer in you," Amy said.

"No lawyer. I'm just someone who had to raise three scrappy kids while trying to keep a ranch going and earning some sort of a profit. You learn how to put out potential fires before they get started," he told her with a wink.

"You do have a lot of skills," Amy said with unabashed admiration.

Connor had no idea what possessed him to look down into her incredibly tempting upturned face and murmur, "You have no idea."

Nor could he have said what spurred him on to do what he did next.

Because one minute they were just talking, shooting the breeze like two very old friends who knew one another well enough to finish each other's sentences, and then the next minute, somehow those same lips that were responsible for making those flippant quips had found their way to hers.

And just like that, with no warning, he was kissing her.

Kissing Amy the way he had always wanted to from perhaps the very first moment he had laid eyes on her all those years ago.

And the kiss turned out to be better than he'd thought it would be.

Way better.

It wasn't a case of just lips meeting lips, it was soul meeting soul.

Before Connor knew it, his arms had slipped around her, all but literally sweeping her off her feet and pulling her against him.

Into him.

The kiss deepened as he felt his pulse accelerating. He knew he shouldn't be doing this, not yet, not when she was still this vulnerable.

But despite his trying to talk himself out of it, it felt as if everything in his whole life had been leading to this very moment, and it would somehow be against the natural order of things if he didn't at least allow himself to enjoy this for a single, shimmering moment in time.

Don't miss A BABY FOR CHRISTMAS
by Marie Ferrarella, available December 2017
wherever Harlequin® Western Romance books
and ebooks are sold.

www.Harlequin.com

THE WORLD IS BETTER
WITH
Romance

Harlequin has everything from contemporary, passionate and heartwarming to suspenseful and inspirational stories.

Whatever your mood,
we have a romance just for you!

Connect with us to find your next great read,
special offers and more.

f /HarlequinBooks

🐦 @HarlequinBooks

www.HarlequinBlog.com

www.Harlequin.com/Newsletters

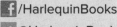